A LIFE APART

MARIAPIA VELADIANO

A LIFE APART

Translated from the Italian by
Cristina Viti

MACLEHOSE PRESS
QUERCUS · LONDON

First published in the Italian language as *La vita accanto*
by Giulio Einaudi editore, Torino, in 2011
First published in Great Britain in 2013 by

MacLehose Press
an imprint of Quercus
55 Baker Street
7th Floor, South Block
London W1U 8EW

A CIP catalogue record for this book is available
from the British Library.

ISBN (HB) 978 0 85705 233 9
ISBN (Ebook) 978 1 78206 084 0

10 9 8 7 6 5 4 3 2 1

Designed and typeset in Albertina by Libanus Press
Printed and bound in Great Britain by Clays Ltd, St Ives plc

A LIFE APART

One

An ugly woman has no vantage point from which to tell her story. No overall perspective. No objectivity. It is a story told from the corner in which life has pushed us, through the crack left open by fear and shame just enough for us to breathe, just enough for us not to die.

An ugly woman cannot voice her desires. She only knows those she can afford. She honestly does not know whether a tight-fitting crimson dress trimmed with velvet at the low-cut neckline would be more to her taste than the classic, entirely anonymous blue one she usually wears to the theatre, where she always sits in the back row and always arrives at the last minute, just before the lights go out, and always in winter, all the better for her scarf and hat to hide her. Nor does she know whether she would like to eat out or go to the match or walk to Santiago de Compostela or swim in the pool or the sea. An ugly woman's field of possibilities is so restricted that all desire is squeezed out. Because it is not just a matter of being aware of time or the weather or money, just like anyone else has to be: it is about existing all the time on tiptoe, on the far margin of the world.

I am ugly. I mean really ugly.

I am not crippled, and so cannot even be pitied.

I have every piece in its place – only just a little too far to one side, or shorter, or longer, or bigger than might be expected. No point making a list, it would give no idea. Yet sometimes, when in the mood for hurting myself, I stand in front of the mirror and survey a few of these pieces: the hair coarse and black like certain dolls used to have long ago, the snub big toe bent into a squiggle by age, the thin mouth drooping to the left into a sorry grimace each time I attempt a smile. And then my sense of smell. I can smell each and every smell, like an animal.

I was born like this. Pretty as babies, they say. But no, not me. I am an insult to the species, and above all to my gender.

"If she were a man at least," my mother says one day in a whisper, speaking from behind me and startling me. She hardly spoke more than once or twice in a week, quite unexpectedly and never addressing anyone in particular.

She certainly never spoke to my father. He on the other hand would try to talk to her: he told her about his work, about me, about life in town, and brought regards from their friends, for as long as they had friends.

When I was born, my mother began to dress in mourning: her femininity withered away at a stroke, as cruelly and abruptly as Jonah's gourd.

After coming back from hospital she never left the house – never again. In the early days, she would receive many visitors: some came out of friendship, some out of a sense of courtesy magnified by a sort of superstitious and gossipy curiosity: God she's ugly, may it happen to you and not to me. Swathed in dark colours, she remained seated on the white sofa in the salon. No-one knows how she found all those black skirts and blouses, she who had dressed in green and sky-blue since childhood.

Guests were always asked to close the door behind them when they came into my bedroom, where I lay in the cradle. My mother was shielding herself from their comments: "Poor thing! Such misfortune!" "Well, what do you expect, it's the taint!" "Yes, but that was different!" "Mmm! Who knows if she told him the whole story!" "She's from the country, isn't she! They were peasants, and in those parts there's always a way to hush up that sort of thing. Blood is not water!" "Will she be right in the head at least?" "And to think the two of them are so beautiful!"

My father is outstandingly handsome: tall, with dark hair and complexion, and black eyes of such intensity as might draw anyone to yield their soul to him. As for my mother, I do not know. They say she was most beautiful, before. I would only steal a glance at her now and again, when I was sure she could not see me. I was frightened of her hollow expression. Neither did she look at me, and heaven only knows how much I feared and at the same time desired her to do so, and not just to check whether anything might have changed, whether the desperate pleas she had at first addressed to an ever more distant God had somehow worked the miracle.

In truth, though, she did not really believe in the miracle, because her family carried the taint. I know now that it is only a small taint. A minor taint, leaving one's mind, face, beauty and life untouched. But back then, people talked about it as if it were a tragedy. Now and again, an unfortunate child – as they said – would be born. At random, wherever it may be, just like God's grace, like a stone slipped from the hand of a juggler in the highest heavens, amen.

"You can't escape the taint," she says at lunchtime one day, addressing her snow-white dessert saucer. The teaspoon she is holding slams hard against the table and the strawberry jelly shakes, its disgusting smell hitting me like a blow.

In fact she had tried to escape the taint, marrying a handsome, young, healthy man from a family that had been untouched by it as far back as could be remembered, through the history of entire generations. No child with multiple fingers hidden away in the stables for a lifetime, entrusted to faithful servants and in the end mysteriously dead, to everyone's relief.

There was talk of six or seven fingers on both hands, and feet with even more toes. Children crossed with beasts, with the spiders that treacherously stalk around at night until you find them lurking silently next to you: our own fears, fashioned for our distress into animal bodies and legs.

That was how I was born: treacherously, after a charmed pregnancy without any sickness or undue weight gain. My mother had carried me as lightly as a game she could cherish, moving gracefully in her clothes of sky-blue and turquoise – the colour of her sea-wave eyes, as my father would say.

"What are the fingers like?" she asks after the delivery in which she has been breathing and pushing, breathing and pushing, holding on to my father's hand.

"The fingers? Oh the *fingers* are perfect," says the midwife, bewildered that anyone could worry about the fingers in the face of such disaster.

"A girl?"

"A girl."

"I want to see her," my mother says as if barely holding on to the edge of happiness, still scared of falling off.

The midwife is at a loss, her hands full with that unsuitable candidate to the human species whose presence has stunted her thoughts.

"She's not crying," she says quickly. "I'll take her through to the children's ward."

And she runs off with the bare, sorry little squirt that is me wrapped up in the green sheet from the delivery room. My father runs after her: he has not seen me yet, because following my mother's wish he has been there for her as a husband, holding her hand the whole time, and not as a doctor – but he is a gynae-cologist, and he knows something awful has happened.

I know all this, and much more, thanks to Aunt Erminia, father's twin sister.

"I'm a freak of nature too," she says the day I ask her the reason for the hushed murmur that always seems to follow me.

"See? Totally identical to your father, but a woman. Doctors say that's impossible, that I only look like him, because for sure we must come from two separate eggs. But we have the same half-moon birthmark back here, see?"

And she bends her elegant long neck towards me, upturning her shock of black hair. "And three tiny moles clustered together right here," and she lifts her T-shirt to show them, there to the side of her soft navel which has the scent of talcum powder and calendula. "We are one, only split into two." And she laughs, a loud laugh that I like and fear.

My mother was allowed to see me on the following day. She did

11

not say a word. She stood looking at that mistake, at my skewed, crooked head, at the cruel traits she had brought forth. She did not take me in her arms. No-one dared to suggest that she breast-feed me.

When my mother decided to stop receiving visitors, my father took me into his practice rooms. For a few months I remained in the ladies' changing cubicle, in the golden yellow pram she had prepared in good time as she imagined our outings along the porticos of Corso Palladio and on to Piazza dei Signori, and perhaps on cooler days as far up as Monte Berico, to thank the seven founder saints and the Virgin for so much happiness.

Every four hours my father's nurse would give me the bottle, cuddling and stroking me on the head as one would a kitten or a pup. At first he would find fault with that gesture, remarking on it almost absent-mindedly, as he always does when trying to avoid hurting anyone. Then, after a while, he let it pass.

That was, in a way, a sheltered situation for me, because the only people to pass that spot were my father's patients. They all adored him, out of the mixture of closeness and complicity that arises from having to share a certain intimacy. For a while, thanks to a sort of transitive property, I also enjoyed some fragments of that adoration. But it did not last long: my father realised that he was losing his pregnant patients, who all saw in my beastly features the cruel personification of their own fears.

"I think she should go to nursery school," Aunt Erminia suddenly says one evening at supper, some time around my third birthday.

She did not live with us, but since the day I was born she had been coming every day, rushing back from the *conservatoire* where she taught piano and taking over the house: organising work, that is, for the home help on duty that day or, more often than not, running things when the home help was absent.

In fact she seemed to spend most of her time interviewing and dismissing home help candidates: "This one's too young, she's come to make cow eyes at your father." "Screechy voice: she lacks all harmony." "Too strict – she'll treat us like so many soldiers." She was demanding because of me, she said. She was looking for someone who could really love me. Sometimes she thought she had found her, and then formally and solemnly hired her. But that would not last: they all ran away on some excuse or other. Once, as she left, a girl who had stayed on a little longer than the others said something that came very close to the truth:

"There is too much sorrow in this house."

The discussion about nursery school was, as I recall, exceedingly drawn out.

"There is time," my father says.

"She needs to be with other children," Aunt Erminia says, pressing him.

"Not yet." My father looks at me: "She needs some extra . . . days. In a few years she'll have had enough days, and she can go to primary school."

"Little ones are more welcoming, their souls are untrained, they see with fresh eyes. Any friends she might make will be her friends for ever." Anxiety increases her need to emphasise words with slightly theatrical gestures.

I am following the discussion, my whole life on hold. I know about nursery school: Aunt Erminia has told me about that paradise of fun and games and children, where you are free to run around and shout. I cannot understand what dark dangers my father might dread, but I don't care: I feel myself strong enough to face them.

"The child is staying at home," my mother says, spelling out the words clearly and abruptly. And as we all turn to look at her, she flicks a fly away with her hand and carries on eating, her eyes on her plate.

There was never any talk of nursery school again.

As a matter of fact, when I was about one year old, a woman who could really love me had indeed been found – and it was my father who had found her.

Maddalena was one of his patients. She had been in his care through two pregnancies and the births of two lovely children with red hair and fair skin, both of whom she had lost in an accident together with her husband only a few years later.

"She's depressed like a sloth in a bath tub," Aunt Erminia says in exasperation, spreading a hand out in front of herself as if to wave off some horrific vision. "She won't do."

"We'll give it a try," my father says calmly.

And Maddalena stayed.

I thought she was lovely. She trailed a light wake of scent, like mist from the plains. She too had red hair, and the tears that streamed down her face day and night mixed with the freckles on her skin.

"Dry these off as well," I say to her one day as I touch those tiny brown spots. And she bursts out laughing in quick shudders that shake her whole body.

She loved me immediately, with the strength of a need that

must be fulfilled. My graceless nature awakened in her a sense of total protectiveness, the same as she would have lavished on the loved ones she had been unable to shelter from harm.

"She's gushing away like a severed artery," Aunt Erminia says, seeking out extreme imagery to try and convince my father. "She will drain our poor child." And with a wide sweeping gesture she describes an imaginary stream rushing down a valley.

"She loves the child as best she can. The child needs a . . . an affectionate figure." My father is choosing his words carefully, not wanting to disrespect my mother even in her absence. "Actively affectionate, that's the word. And Maddalena is like that."

Maddalena would hold me close and teach me to make cakes, to beat eggs with sugar until they were soft and white like whipped cream, to work the egg whites in a double boiler, puffing them up with a movement as round and smooth as a sea wave.

"Like a treble clef," says Aunt Erminia, half glad, half jealous of this new closeness I am sharing. And she draws a clef in the air.

Aunt Erminia was not maternal, but she was a live wire, an artist. She was without a husband but did not seem to be without men.

"As many as the pilgrims at the *Festa degli Oto* would want to marry her," Maddalena says with the freedom of one who has left that kind of pursuit behind for ever.

Aunt Erminia interrupts: "The only males who go up to Monte Berico for the *Festa degli Oto* are cheats and pimps who want their souls washed clean by the friars, just to be on the safe side. Is that the sort of man you want me to marry?" And she laughs, her head thrown back, her hair shaking like a vague promise.

15

She was indeed very beautiful. Like my father, she had the ability to give herself entirely to anyone who might be in front of her. She would gaze at them with her deep black eyes and at once make them feel very important. She did not talk much, but when she did, secrets stood revealed and things were made to happen: "Today we change colours in the kitchen!" and she lands two tins of yellow paint on the table.

"We are going to Monte Berico. Chop-chop, flat shoes on, off we go!" and she drags me out of the house, right past my mother, who does not answer our greeting.

I only ever went out at night: before supper in winter, after supper in summer. I was late understanding that my aunt had to wait until after dark. My seclusion had been ordered by my mother: going out was taboo, a taboo invisibly sculpted in the elegantly marbled walls of the house, a taboo on which the residue of life left inside would stand or fall.

We would take the dimly lit, deserted street between the two rivers. The smell of river weeds changed with the seasons: sweetish in summer, sharper in winter. Then we would climb up the flight of steps to Monte Berico, or sometimes go by the lower route, along the porticos. Always running, breathless, all the way up to the Piazzale, so we could look at the city below.

"It's huge," I say, pointing at the dark shapes of houses and blocks under construction down below. "How do people find their homes?"

"All you have to do is keep the reference points." And Aunt Erminia has me line my eye with her index finger as she points to the Basilica Palladiana with its green cupola swelling over Piazza dei Signori, or pans around to the façade of San Lorenzo or the Bissara Tower, "That's going to topple like a pyramid of peanuts one of these days."

"Will you take me to see it one day?"

"You can see much better from here."

Sometimes her pointing finger would fix on one palazzo and she would tell me about its history, kneaded with the owners' clandestine love affairs, the mysterious deaths of servants and unwanted witnesses, the lavish gifts of some more generous scion, the fortunate alliances, the disastrous collapses.

"History is nothing but vintage gossip, and don't you forget it," she says laughing as the perfume of her hair splashes over me and cuts my breath short.

She knew those palazzos one by one. Over time I learnt that she had some friend or admirer in each and every one of them. She attracted men with the excessive beauty of a dark complexion that evoked exotic sensualities, with her girlish long hair, with her laugh that exploded like a loud feast. And with music. Aunt Erminia was hardly outstanding as a musician, but few of her followers listened to her playing: hers was music for the eyes. Some critics were quite harsh with her: one evening, laughing, she read out one review to me: ". . . beyond the dazzling physicality of the pianist there is little more than the skill of a well-educated amateur." But audiences adored her, and in the provinces she was a celebrity.

Whenever she spoke, Aunt Erminia would move her hands in the air, looking like a conductor fashioning a harmony of words rather than notes. She had perfect hands: her long, slender fingers

17

would fan out to clarify some important concept, bunch up in a nervous fist to emphasise an idea, or cut a horizontal slash in front of someone's eyes to close a discussion. They were bewitching hands to look at, and whenever Aunt Erminia was playing they would glide so lightly over the piano keys as to make one wonder whether the strings were being touched by some faraway magic.

I soon learnt to gesticulate as she did, with no need for any practice: I learnt out of affection, out of my desire to be like her. And so our conversations came to resemble a sort of comical hand ballet that might have looked from a distance like some secret sign language created to exclude the rest of the world.

All of a sudden, in the middle of one of our conversations, Aunt Erminia grabs hold of my wrists and looks at my hands as if for the first time:

"But they're wonderful!" she says.

And then, to my father:

"The child must play. She has a musician's hands. I've been blind!"

And without the slightest pause she drags me over to the piano:

"Play!" she orders.

"Play what?" I say. I am frightened. I have never dared to touch the baby grand on which she and my father play most evenings, sitting side by side, their shoulders touching lightly, their hands alike, elegant and self-assured, chasing each other without touching, coming closer and moving apart, interweaving and leaving each other, resting on the final note, ending with sadness, then one starting again quite unexpectedly and the other renewing the chase, wasting each other with pleasure, meandering lost among the notes as if it were for ever.

"Play anything you like. Be a cat on the keys: go for a stroll."

And I stroll at random up and down the keyboard. I know its unmistakable smell of antique wood treated with preserving oils, the low and high notes: they too are graceless at first but then I go back and correct them, I too am chasing a music, a little music of my own. Aunt Erminia can see something in my fingers:

"You will be a wonderful pianist!" and she scoops me up in an embrace. Then she sits at the piano and, tossing her head back, plays an *impromptu* that sets the walls shaking.

Music took hold of my life. The entirely new awareness that something was expected of me filled my days with feelings I had not known, feelings that took the place of that sort of empty waiting that had held my energies frozen until then. Perhaps I could show that something in me was good after all, that I could be loved in my own right rather than out of some hazy sense of protectiveness or guilt.

I was not the child prodigy that Aunt Erminia had seen, but I learnt quickly, and wanted to play with my whole being.

For a long time my father kept quiet. In the evening, after supper, he would stand behind me and listen, and I could feel his black eyes piercing my hands. I could feel his uncertain thoughts, how he feared deluding himself and in turn causing me to delude myself.

Later he took to listening to me as he sat in the little white cretonne armchair next to the turquoise glazed earthenware stove. He would not speak or offer any advice, but he was relaxed: I could see him close his eyes and follow the music's rhythm with imperceptible movements of his fingers.

I have been playing from memory ever since the first day. In fact my memory was quite unused, the idle waste of my days hardly taking up a fragment of it. Reading a score once was enough for me to remember it as easily as the prayers Maddalena would teach me at night. That way I was able to look at my hands: I would watch them in amazement as they created the sounds that filled the air, follow them as they took on a life of their own, leaving the body, gliding over the keys, stopping at the pauses, teasing out the grace notes and slowing at the finale. Just like Papa's hands, just like Aunt Erminia's.

At first, Aunt Erminia herself was my teacher. She would come in the morning or in the evening, depending on her teaching schedule at the *conservatoire*. In winter I would wait for her with my nose squashed against the glass pane of the salon window, in summer I would slip my head between the slender stone columns of the balcony. By the time she came, I would have already spent several hours playing, but I never let her find me sitting at the piano. I would run to meet her, and she would scoop me up, lift me high, and then set me down on the stool.

"Light, light, light!" she says, improvising a swift arabesque on the keys.

"Or heavy, heavy, heavy!" she roars, swooping thunderously on the lower notes.

And we began. After a while Maddalena would come in, bringing tea, freshly baked meringues, the vanilla biscuits I loved, the *gâteau au beurre*. Then we would go and ask my mother, who until that moment had remained in her room on the opposite side of the house, to come and take afternoon tea with us. She never spoke, but I took care to leave the doors open in the hope she might be listening and would one day say something about my progress.

"The child must be enrolled at the *conservatoire*," Aunt Erminia says one evening at suppertime, abruptly dropping her spoon and clenching her fist as if to stop that thought escaping her. "She's below the normal age for auditions, but exceptions are made for a talent such as hers."

My father rests his fork and places his hands palms down on the table, with the gesture used for important discussions that require patience. He struggles for words, without looking at me.

"She is going to school in October and heaven knows how . . . how difficult that will be. The *conservatoire*, with all those little girls in their pretty white shirts and pleated navy skirts, the ribbon in their hair bobbing up and down in time with the 'Rondo alla Turca' – that would be . . . too much, just too much."

Aunt Erminia explodes, crackling like green wood in the fireplace:

"She's not some 'Rondo alla Turca' piano player! She is a pianist made for the *impromptu* and *polonaise*, for the 'Wanderer Fantasie', for Rachmaninov! She can transform music, she can make it . . . make it beautiful. She has people in tears when she plays, you know that! She's without equal in her age group – like a prodigy. And you cannot ignore a miracle!"

Maddalena passes me the pudding, weeping all the while in her open and generous manner. I only have a vague idea of what is wrong with me. I know I am ugly, very ugly. My frightening ugliness is a shadow walking in front of me – but I cannot imagine what it might become once set outside the walls of the house.

"I'll wear skirts and ribbons too, if I must," I hasten to say. But no-one replies.

The only sound comes from my mother, who is toying with the excessively red, excessively round cherry decorating the pudding on her china saucer.

I enrolled in the *conservatoire* much later, five years later in fact. I sat my exam, just as my father had predicted, among excruciatingly pretty little girls in ribbons and bows. But in the meantime, horrifying things had happened in my life, and by then I knew. I played behind a tall wooden door as highly polished as the marble slab behind the Madonna of Monte Berico where people lay their hands to beg for grace, on a flat-sounding piano that was much inferior to mine. I knew, I had learnt: while playing, I must remain expressionless, for the best expression on my face is precisely no expression at all. I must pour my entire life into my hands – all of my life, all of it.

The examiners remained locked in discussion for a whole hour, Aunt Erminia with them. I had played very well, and was much more advanced than all those little girls. I knew by now what they would be discussing: they were wondering whether a creature of such unfortunate appearance would ever be able to play, what she would be able to make of her art, what point there was in training – I beg your pardon, I mean "cultivating" her. This is what they were saying, choosing their words carefully so as to show no disrespect to Aunt Erminia.

"Ten out of ten. You're in!" Aunt Erminia says, rushing out and wringing her hands. It is her turn to cry, but not for joy.

Maddalena leads me away from the corridor where I have been waiting between two rows of candidates, all stiff and silent next to their mothers.

"What shall I do now?" I say as I stand still outside the main gate of the *conservatoire*, holding on to Maddalena's hand as if it were a safety ring.

I have grown, and she can no longer take me up in her arms as she used to, so she hugs me, but not like one would hug a little girl: it feels as if she too is holding on for safety. Forgetting that I am only ten years old, she says:

"You shall play, my girl, that's what. And you shall eat and sleep and go places. Life must be taken wholesale, if you start nitpicking that's the end of it. You shall play and play and play. That's your gift, and there are those born without even one single little gift to go by."

That was what she said, more or less – in a sharp voice, but blowing her nose from weeping with the emotion.

Back home we found my father sitting in one of the little armchairs in the hall, a medical journal in his hands.

"Back already, Doctor?" Maddalena says sternly.

"How did it go?"

"Very well, of course: she was admitted."

That word sounds and feels like a promise of life coming towards me. Admitted: there is a place for me, all for me, and I have won it. I have not turned up at the *conservatoire* like some misfortune come out of the blue.

My excitement speaks for me:

"But will you do with me what you do with Aunt Erminia?"

"Do what?" my father says, staring straight at me.

"Play four-hand in the evening," I say through my fear.

"We shall see," he says, gently, after a moment.

Two

The ancient two-storey palazzo overlooking the Retrone river, in the old neighbourhood of Le Barche, had been bought by my father shortly before his marriage, and lovingly restored by my mother. All the rooms had high narrow windows, many with little balconies in Vicenza stone, a brittle material requiring continual maintenance. Apart from the salon on the first floor, the house was always plunged in half-shadow. For that reason my mother had chosen only pastel colours for the walls and the furnishings. She loved light blue, and had been forced to engage in lengthy negotiations by the town planning authority, who had decreed the balconies must be green, like those in the other palazzos of the city – but she did have her way in the end, opting for a pale lava blue that she described in the application paperwork as sage green.

The salon was huge. Two of its outer walls overlooked the still, dark waters of the Retrone, and six French windows reaching all the way up to the ceiling let the light in. Each window had a gauzy white curtain, with a heavier one, sky-blue and edged with silver threads, hanging over it to give shade on hot summer days. One of the windows opened onto a corner balcony that led to my parents' bedroom – or rather, since the day of my birth, my father's bedroom. The world's bustle disturbed my mother, who had moved into a room at the back of the house, overlooking the river.

The ground floor was taken up by the kitchen, the dining-room, a study and a small drawing-room sited exactly below the salon balcony. This was the coolest room in the house, and in summer my mother spent her days there, sitting in an armchair upholstered in a Sanderson fabric printed with a pattern of violet and blue hydrangeas. She often held a book in her hands, but hardly ever seemed to turn the pages. Returning from his clinic or from the hospital, my father would go to her as she sat in that room, and speak to her.

I would listen to him from the balcony. Hidden away from passers-by thanks to the balustrade and an oleander plant, I sat hugging my knees and leaning my back against the sharp corner – and I waited. When the season made it necessary to close the windows, I sat listening instead on the first step of the inside staircase.

I could hear my father coming in:

"Good evening to my lady!" he would say every single day.

He would sit in front of her and take her hands into his. I never really saw what happened, but I did hear every sound and could easily imagine.

He would tell her about his work: his patients, their pregnancies and childbirths, their illnesses, their problems, his doubts. Often he would answer himself, his voice now deep, now tense, now just tinged with gladness when a high-risk situation had been resolved, when a mother had been saved. I would listen very closely to everything he said: his low voice would slide along my body like an embrace, and his rolling r's had the effect of a caress that reached deep inside me to some sensitive spot in my mind, numbing it into a sort of blank, weightless abandon. There was something of a secret in the pathway of his words, and I thought he always sought those that best highlighted the deep vibration of his voice. I could feel his voice inside me, it stayed with me all through the night and the following day, until the next night, the renewed meeting. Sometimes my father would also speak to her about me, and then I would listen to his words with even closer attention: he told her that I played very well, that I was already writing my own music, that I seemed to be at ease.

"It's happening tomorrow," he says to her on the evening before my first day at school. In my bedroom, the light blue school bag is ready, with all its pens, crayons and pencils. With the required exercise books in their dust jackets: red, green, yellow and blue. With the little rounded scissors and the wooden ruler. With Aunt Erminia's present: a light blue and white fountain pen with a nib of white gold.

It is the last day of September, a day that still holds the sultry heat coming from the plains of the Po. A slightly sickening smell of old river weeds is rising from the water.

The words are brand new and the r's in my father's throat seem to slip away as if sucked back into a whirlpool.

"She's going out tomorrow. I know you must be worried. You'd like to keep her at home – and so would I, perhaps. But we can't, we mustn't. Good God, how I want you to be here for me, with me, at times like these! Look at me for once! Do you remember when you used to tell me my black eyes held the whole universe, when I used to answer that the universe was blue as your eyes, not black like mine! I know you're in there. Say something, speak to me. I know you don't want her to go out, I know. I did as you wished:

no nursery school, no *conservatoire*. But we can't now, do you understand?"

I can hear him shaking her. Perhaps he has grabbed her by the shoulders. No poetry. When he speaks to her, my father turns into a poet and addresses her as if in verse – but not tonight.

"Erminia says you're like a walled-up fortress – but she doesn't know you the way I do. You're a wall of fire, but burn only inside. God how I miss you tonight. What shall we do? Should we have beastly figures carved out of stone and place them at the front door like the dwarves of Villa Valmarana, and keep her locked up in here with her tutors, like they used to do back then? Perhaps it is life after all, the way you live inside this house, perhaps more of a life than mine out there. What do I take from the outside in the end? My life is here. And I am so inadequate! Do you understand? Yet I do have some happiness to cherish: I did know happiness with you! And I still hope . . . but she . . . what can *she* hold and cherish if we keep her shut inside? You will say it's better to live with desire than with relentless humiliation. Better locked up in the misfits' palace rather than free to be mocked, excluded and wounded?"

I sink my head between my knees and press until it hurts. Maddalena had told me that story: a dwarf princess had been born at the Villa Valmarana, and her parents had always kept her locked inside the house, employing dwarf servants, dwarf jugglers and dwarf tutors so that she would be spared the sorrow of knowing her condition. But one day the princess had somehow been able to look over the high wall surrounding the villa and to look at the world below. And climbing the narrow cobbled street was the most beautiful prince, the easy stride of his supple long legs swirling the folds of his soft cloak around his perfect body. Then the dwarf princess, overcome by despair, threw herself into the street below and died. When the seventeen servants of the villa looked over the wall and saw that their princess had come to such a gruesome end, they were turned to stone with grief – and there they still are, seventeen statues of sorrow.

"I know that all of this would be no tragedy," my father says, his voice growing more and more strained, "if only we were together. But to be unable to understand what has stolen away your soul at a stroke! It wasn't the child, no, it wasn't. I see mothers every day who adore their disadvantaged children as if they were so many Child Christs. Our child is . . . she's a prodigy. I mean it! She is our child. She carries our lives inside her, and we can help her find her own. How can you not see? Your sea-wave eyes are always so far away. I would want to look even just once where you are looking, and to understand where your sorrow comes from: I might be able to fight a sickness that I know."

There is a noise behind me: Maddalena. She puts her index finger to her lips and takes me by the hand. Downstairs, the noise has startled my father, and I can hear the swish of the armchair fabric. From the way she is holding me, I can tell that Maddalena has been listening. Perhaps she too always listens.

"You will go to school and do very well," she says firmly as she drags me away. "And the more time you spend with your head and heart out of this house the better. Remember you are the only proper person in here – the only one."

"What about my father? What about Aunt Erminia?" I say as tears begin to well inside me.

"Satan can also dress up as an angel of light," Maddalena says, sharp and dry as an oracle. But seeing how frightened I am she corrects herself:

"Sometimes we have to be careful even of those who love us."

Three

Of course I have a name: it is Rebecca. But I only really found out on the first day at school, when Miss Albertina started to call me by my name – and she has never stopped.

Maddalena's sweaty hand had almost crushed my fingers as we made our way. When I let go of it to take Miss Albertina's dry hand, I thought that the teacher had surely never cried in her whole life.

She was short, slightly built, her straight black bob emphasising her every word with sharp movements in a sort of shiver.

"She is late. Are you the mother?" she says as she takes my hand. I see her hair start sharply backwards as she looks up at Maddalena, who is at least eight inches taller. We are outside the classroom. A subdued buzz of voices is coming from behind the door.

"No I'm not ... actually ... her mother is ... she's not well. Her father is a doctor, he ... he had an emergency this morning ... just this morning, very early." Maddalena is stammering and telling lies, at least about my father: he was ready at our front door, austere and elegant in his blue linen trousers and monogrammed white shirt, then he decided that she should take me.

The teacher's hair quivers with a tinge of annoyance.

"Would you tell them that I should be delighted to meet them. Have a good day."

"Yes of course ... I shall tell them today ... as soon as I get back.

Straight away." I hear Maddalena's reply, which only reaches the teacher's back.

I know now that dying of grief really is quite hard, and not worth hoping for – but that morning, when I walked into the classroom with its endlessly high ceiling, that had suddenly become quiet as a cathedral, I did hope with all my strength that my poor unfortunate body, pierced by the darting eyes of those twenty-two motionless children, would reach its end.

But no. Miss Albertina's hair fell rigorously straight at the sides of her stern face as she moved some of the girls so as to place me where she thought might be best: in the third row, next to the wall, right by the window. I had no-one behind me, but could see everyone, and above all, sense everyone. I could not hear their words, that had been tamed in good time by Miss Albertina – but I could feel their heavy thoughts and smell their curiosity as it oozed from the excited skin of their hands that were covering their mouths, hiding their grimacing.

Next to me sat a blonde, fair-skinned, hugely fat girl.

"My name is Lu-cil-la," she whispers, almost without moving her mouth. "You are Rebecca, the daughter of my Mamma's doctor. I saw you once in his study, a few months ago: you were with your Mamma, she has won-der-ful red hair. The teacher is my aunt. She's my Mamma's sister but they're very different. My Mamma is like me – fat, I mean. But we must thank God, because everything's alright with us: our legs and our brains, I mean. We mustn't grumble about the way we are: it could be much worse. She says I talk too much but I've promised her I'll be ve-ry-qui-et in class. Aunt Albertina is ve-ry-strict but ve-ry-good, my Mamma says. Of course she was ab-so-lu-tely against me being in her class, because we're related obviously, but my Mamma did everything she could, you must have a good education she says. Very high ceilings, aren't they? This school's real-ly-an-cient, but I live nearby, so Mamma doesn't have to take me. You live nearby too – that's why you're also coming here, isn't it?"

Lucilla was the first person outside the family I had ever come into contact with: I was not even sure whether it would be proper to call her by her first name.

"Well? You might answer, you know. Are you worried we'll get told off? All you have to do is not move your lips – and she's not looking anyway. And besides, what can she do to us? She can hard-ly-kill-us."

Perhaps my father had not taken me because he had decided that I should begin to face the world alone, without the protection coming from his elegant and authoritative persona – or perhaps he had been scared. Scared of his own fear and mine. But I was more alone than I could bear to be.

I cannot say what might have pushed Lucilla to be my friend from the very first day. At times I have thought it might be because of her physical otherness, but I was wrong. She saw herself as beautiful, and in her very special way she really was. Ours has never been a pathetic sum of two misfortunes but a true friendship, born and nurtured at first only thanks to her, since I felt and was utterly unfit for any social relationship. I was unable to answer her that day. I lacked the words to voice my thoughts, perhaps I even lacked the thoughts. No-one had ever sought my opinion on anything, or asked me whether I had been to nursery school, or how my days were spent. But I did answer Miss Albertina when she asked me, as she had done with all the other children, what I knew about our city. I spoke to her of Corso Palladio, that runs south-west to north-east across the town centre following the line of the ancient *decumanus*, and of Corso Fogazzaro and Contrà Porte, vying for recognition as the ancient *cardo maximus* and dividing urban spaces into a grid that was not always orderly, owing to the presence of the streams that have always graced, and sometimes threatened and destroyed, the life of the city. I spoke of the Basilica Palladiana that casts its austere, watchful countenance over the square where gentlemen and ladies rub shoulders with the poor on festive days. And also of the Basilica at Monte Berico, cradling the secrets of an entire city deep inside the cross-stitched *ex-voto* hearts and the flames of the candles lit by those who climb to the top to pray for grace, as Aunt Erminia had told me. But still I was at a loss when she asked me what I liked best about those monuments. I knew their histories, their outline against the evening sky, their position on the city map, the gossip that had been growing around them through the ages. But I had never seen them.

"Not even Corso Palladio?" Miss Albertina says.

"No," I reply.

"Each one of you should feel like an important person here," says Miss Albertina, finally smiling as the bell sounds and it is time to say goodbye. "Some of you might do better than others. Some might understand maths better, some others might be very good at drawing. But you are all clever enough to respect one another, you can all be polite, you can all learn to be generous, and there is absolutely no reason to accept any slacking on this point. Agreed?"

Miss Albertina always looked at me too: her eyes did not shy away, and neither did they scan the folds of my features in curiosity.

That day at the school gate I found Aunt Erminia looking dazzling: she was wearing a long, tight dress, teal green with a thin gold thread at the neckline, the sleeves and the hem. She was beautiful – much too beautiful for the time and the place.

"Your father behaved shamefully," she says, scooping me up and kissing me as she always does. "I steamrollered him like a cat under a juggernaut. Leaving you all alone this morning. All alone! How could anyone do that?"

Back home my father was sitting in an armchair in the dining-room, the smart clothes he was wearing in the morning still in perfect order. He had just come back from work, he said, but his briefcase was still at the bottom of the stairs, where I had seen it on my way to school. He probably had not left the house at all. He looked up as I came in and hinted at a movement with his back, as if to stand up and come to meet me. But he stopped, scanning my face for the answer to his fears.

"Indecent," Aunt Erminia says as she furiously hurls her handbag onto the table.

"What is?" my father says in alarm. "The school?"

"Well, if you really want to know," Aunt Erminia replies as she storms past him with a harsh clicking of heels, "you are!"

Remorse and rage gave them both the chance to omit asking me about my first day at school.

At the table I suddenly felt like opening the windows. I stood up without asking permission and began with the dining-room windows. I did it slowly, partly because they were high and heavy and I could hardly reach. Then I went into the little drawing-room – two windows. Then the study and the kitchen – four more. On my way upstairs I flung wide the door of the little landing balcony and felt the rush of air coming from the river. Then I went into the salon – six French windows – then into my bedroom – two windows, and two for each of the other rooms. I was counting them out loud: twenty-four in all.

"It's draughty," Mamma says, staring down at her plate.

"Never mind," I say as I return to my place and with a sideways glance catch sight of my father and Maddalena, who both at the same time stop short from getting up and closing the windows again.

"Well done," Maddalena says, drying her tears, as we stand in the kitchen afterwards. "We need some fresh air in here."

That day I played all afternoon with the windows of the salon open wide over the river and the curtains whipped into a wild dance by a rainstorm that no longer felt like summer.

"They're getting wet," Maddalena says, standing at a loss in the middle of the room.

"Like the sails of a ship," I say, raising my voice slightly.

"Have you ever seen one?"

"No, I haven't."

"Then I'll take you to Venice this Sunday."

"In the daytime?"

"In the daytime."

"They won't let me."

"Yes they will! You opened the windows, didn't you?"

"But are there sailing ships in Venice?"

"Perhaps a few little sailboats. And liners, cruising ships. And gondolas with little seats of red velvet with golden tassels. They slide away, silent as tears."

"How many people are there in Venice?"

"The whole world."

"Then we can go."

I did not go to Venice that Sunday. After sleeping all week with my bedroom windows open wide to the damp cold of the river, I fell ill and was forced to stay in bed for a few days.

That was my first illness, and turned out to be as instructive as it was pleasant. My father looked after me, and above all would stay up late to play chess with me, neglecting his monologues with Mamma. Aunt Erminia gave me a record player and a little yellow rocking chair to sit in as I listened to music. Maddalena brought me meals in bed and kissed me on the forehead at regular intervals on the pretext of checking my temperature.

"It's nice to be ill," I say to her in the evening.

"It is at first. But after a while people get fed up. Compassion is like fish: after three days it rots."

On the third day Lucilla came to visit. She appeared on the threshold of my bedroom door in mid-afternoon one day, looking enormous in a white tracksuit.

"Hi. I should have an-noun-ced-my-self, as my Mamma says – but I don't have your phone number, and it's not listed. And anyway, I thought it would be ab-so-lu-tely impossible for you to be out if you're ill. Maybe you don't feel like talking, in which case tell me straight-a-way and I'll disappear. Your Mamma was e-ver-so-kind. She kissed me again and again, and said that I was blessed: could she have been crying? And she told me to come up – oh, I saw your grandma too, on my way up: she was sitting in a room next to the staircase. Perhaps I should have gone up to her, but I wasn't sure that would be the right thing. My Mamma says I must-not-be-a-nuis-ance, and that what counts is doing the right thing."

Hard to imagine anyone who at her young age could be so far from doing the right thing according to common manners. I explained who Maddalena was, and also Aunt Erminia, the lady she sometimes saw waiting for me at the school gate. But I did not dare tell her that the dark, forlorn figure sitting in the little armchair was my mother.

"Where is your mother then?" she asks, leaning over the bed until her head nearly touches my pillow.

"She's not well," I say quickly.

"Is she in hospital?"

"No, she isn't."

But Lucilla was as curious as she was gluttonous. When she got back to her house after eating the vanilla biscuits that Maddalena had brought for us that afternoon, she must have pestered her mother until she finally got to know what the whole town already knew. And so, the next day, she launched into a new sally:

"My Mamma used to know your mother well, before she ... got ill. She says she was beautiful and gentle. Somewhat artistic. She says you won't talk about her because you might be ashamed of her. But you mustn't be. You are yourself, she says. You're doing very well, you can read and write already, you can play the piano. And then, you have your father, your Aunt Erminia. I don't have a father and it's cer-tain-ly-bet-ter that way, seeing as we're the talk of the town because of him."

I was not wounded by Lucilla. It was impossible to take against such an abundance of good will. Her empathy made her unimpeachable. I did not take offence, but had no wish to talk about my mother, and so listened with relief to her account of her father's misdeeds: he was a two-ti-mer and a pae-do-phile, two new words enticing my childish curiosity, unaccustomed as I was to any sharing of secrets.

Until Lucilla came into my life, the boundaries of my world had coincided exactly with those of my house: the river at the back, and the neighbourhood of Le Barche, that I knew only from my night escapades with Aunt Erminia, in front: narrow, dark, mostly deserted streets. Lucilla did not have the power to make me beautiful, even though with her I have at times forgotten my ugliness – but she succeeded in shifting my horizon a little further, expanding it to reach her house, which was hardly a few hundred yards away, but appeared to my eyes like a universe seen through a looking-glass. And not only because her house – a three-bedroom flat with a dark narrow corridor, fully taken up by herself and her mother with their ample forms – was tiny compared to mine, or because the kitchen had pink walls and purple fixtures that matched the bathroom tiles or the bedroom curtains. None of the rules and laws that I knew was respected in that house.

Lucilla was free to leave her jersey thrown on a footstool in the hall, her school bag in the kitchen, her shoes in the bedroom. She was free to scatter traces of herself wherever she went, to vent anger at her mother if she was not allowed another ice cream or a new book. She was free to ask and free to exist. My own existence on the other hand was stained with a sort of original debt due to my horrible ugliness, something that made it natural for me to have no claim to anything more than the miraculous affection that my father, Aunt Erminia and Maddalena were able to feel for me. I was grateful for that, drenched as it were in a sorrowful gratitude that reached so deep into my feelings and desires as to allow them expression only when they perfectly coincided with those of the people around me. But back then I had no way of knowing that, and so would look on in amazement as Lucilla threw a tantrum, or hold my breath listening to the swarm of words with which her mother would chase her around the house. I was frightened by the quantity of feelings that could be expressed in words. In my house, words were as flat as dictionary entries, and were hardly ever used to convey anything other than information, engagements, appointments. On a very few occasions, when the talk was of myself and my future, Aunt Erminia would grow animated and fall with my father into brief skirmishes which would end in a sort of spent agreement.

At Lucilla's, words would swell with rage, grow long and spiky as hatpins, bare their teeth, sink them into the soul, fret and fume, and sometimes explode into screams that would deform them past all meaning. Or else, and sometimes immediately afterwards, unexpectedly, while shock and sorrow still shook the limbs, words would grow lighter, less turgid, and open out into a soothing, cool caress that brought the dispute to a close.

"Good heavens, you're soaked!"

On my first visit, Lucilla's mother opens the door, her body squashed against the door frame, taking up the whole space. Even the corners seem to bulge with the fullness of her. She is wearing an enormous yellow raincoat covered in perfectly spherical droplets. Tiny pink piglets are jingling in front of my eyes and dripping water onto the floor.

This is also the first time I have left the house on my own, and the anxious exhortations to take good care repeated by Maddalena up to the moment of our goodbye outside the house are jostling with a generous range of polite greetings, which have no way of getting through the stream of words coming from Lucilla's mother.

"Ah yes, I've just come in myself," she says hurriedly. "I've still not put my brolly down, see?" And I notice that the piglets are in fact dangling from the spokes of a huge acid-green umbrella.

"These were made of clay originally – imagine," she explains. "They all went to pieces in the first rainstorm, so I've replaced them with these little rubber ones. Not as pretty of course, but very practical. Oh – please do come in, darling, come in, sweetheart!"

And I think I will never be able to get in, because there is not space enough for anyone else in that hall. But she takes my hand, squeezes and squashes herself against me and ushers me into a short narrow corridor where my boots are placed on a small mat, my little umbrella inside a white floor rack shaped like acanthus leaves, my raincoat on a wooden stand meant to look like a man with raised arms. And there is space for Lucilla too, when she comes from her bedroom teetering perilously on the spiky heels of a pair of huge pea-green shoes with white polka dots.

"Make yourself at home!" Lucilla's Mamma shouts a moment later from the kitchen, where she is putting a fruit tart in the oven and at the same time, her hands still dusted with flour, hammering on the keys of a garish red typewriter the translations from English and German by which she makes a living.

And I did, sitting very properly in the little orange director's chair in Lucilla's bedroom as she settled herself cross-legged on the bed and tried to start an ever-broken tape recorder, at the same time telling me once again about her father who had eloped a couple of years earlier with a ve-ry-beau-tiful and scandalously young girl after pulverising the bank account and selling the house on the sly. Dis-ap-peared, dis-solved without a trace. The whole town had been talking about it, had I not heard? No, I had not.

"She was one of his students," Lucilla says, whispering so as not to be overheard by her mother. "My father taught Greek and Latin at the Liceo Pigafetta. They had been lovers for two years, in secret because she was un-der-age – imagine. Then, as soon as she turned eighteen, they dis-ap-peared. One morning she left for school, and so did he. Then, nothing. My mother found herself on her own with a small child – me, that is. Her work doesn't pay well enough, so she swallowed her pride and reported him: the police are still looking for him. Because of the main-tenance, you understand."

I did not understand much at all, but listened to the story of a different life and compared it to mine: what is better, a cheating father who in the end disappears altogether, or a mother who is there but also is not, so that you may perhaps still hope for something and spend your life frozen in wait?

"It was a re-al-re-lief for us," says Lucilla, who evidently has absorbed her mother's words to the point of becoming one with her. "The last years had been she-er-hell: he would shout at my mother that she was fat and stupid and had only been able to have a little girl as fat and stupid as herself. He would tell her she was ignorant because she did not read phil-os-ophy and knew nothing about Noh theatre. And Mamma would stand up for me, saying I am a sen-sitive child, that I have a gift for singing, that you must look for the right-qua-lities in a person."

She spoke with no sorrow, patiently shaking the tape recorder until it started with a jarring hiss that hardly allowed a hint of the sound to come through. A music genre that was never heard at my house, where no-one cared for singing: *Lieder* that sounded mournful and brilliant in equal measure to my young ears, sung in German and therefore incomprehensible. She would sing over the recorded voices and make up the German words she did not know. She would obsessively repeat one stanza from Schubert's "Die Forelle": "so zuckte seine Rute, das Fischlein zappelt dran, und ich mit regem Blute sah die Betrog'ne an."

"The fisherman tugged hard on his line, the little fish was thrashing, and I looked on in sorrow at the poor de-ceived-victim," Lucilla says, translating for me each time, reciting from memory the version her mother has written out for her on old exercise book pages.

"Why 'deceived'?" I ask, playing along with her game.

"Because the fisherman, to catch the little fish swimming happily in the clear little brook, had mud-died-the-water. The rogue," she says, bringing her hands up to her face and opening her eyes wide to emphasise the horror of that act.

At other times she would bend her powerful childish voice to the drama of "Gretchen am Spinnrade": "mein Busen drängt sich nach ihm hin. Ach dürft ich fassen un halten ihn, und küssen ihn, so wie ich wollt, an seinen Küssen vergehen sollt!"

"My breast is yearning for him – ah, would that I could hold him, and keep him, and kiss him just as I want, no matter if I die-of-his-kis-ses!" Lucilla repeats over and over again, hugging her generous body, her head tilted over one shoulder and her eyes closed.

I preferred Gregorian chant: there was something familiar in those Latin sounds, reminding me of the prayers Maddalena would recite for me at bedtime. I loved them because they were gentle and sounded like lullabies.

I would listen without replying. I liked it when the talk was not about me: sorrow touching someone else was such a relief that I felt no guilt or embarrassment.

What astonished me about Lucilla was the relative poverty in which she lived. I noticed, without understanding, that no-one would see to replacing old or broken things like the tape recorder, or the pencil case that would not zip up, or the pencil stubs so short that they would slip out from between her fingers.

When, at home, she took her shoes off, my gaze would fall

again and again on her fat toes poking out of socks that might once have been pink or light blue.

Sometimes she would notice:

"Mamma says I eat-through-socks and she can't keep up. This month she's had to buy me all-of-the-ex-ercise books for school. Just as well I was given all the textbooks by my aunt – though I shouldn't tell any-one, or they'll think she's being unfair."

Four

Being born ugly is like being born with a chronic illness that can only worsen with age. At no time in life does the future promise to be any better than the present, there are no happy memories from which to derive any consolation, and to give oneself up to dreams results only in a surplus of sorrow.

An ugly child lives warily, striving to behave in such ways as would not add to the trouble already caused by her appearance. An ugly child will not throw tantrums or make demands, will learn very quickly to eat without dropping breadcrumbs, will play quietly and only shift things when strictly necessary, will tidy her room without being asked, will not be caught twice biting her fingernails, will not wear out socks and shoes because she moves very carefully, will not raise her voice or make a noise as she goes downstairs, will not argue about which clothes to wear.

An ugly child is grateful to everyone for any affection they may show her despite the disappointment of her birth, she knows her place, says thank you for the presents that are just what she wanted, is always happy of anything that may be proposed to her, seeks no attention or caresses, keeps herself in good health: since she cannot give any pleasure or satisfaction, she will at least try to cause no trouble.

An ugly child will see, observe, investigate, listen, perceive, grasp by intuition; in each inflection of a voice, each facial expression, each gesture that might escape control, each brief or drawn-out silence, she seeks some token element that may concern her, for good or for bad. She is frightened of hearing anything that may confirm what she already knows: that her life is a real misfortune. She is always hoping to hear one word that will absolve her, even if it should be spoken merely out of pity.

An ugly child is the daughter of chance, fatality, destiny, a freak of nature. She is surely not a child of God.

"The priest is here," Maddalena says, rushing breathlessly into the kitchen where we are having lunch. Our doorbell very seldom rings. "He's sorry to come at such an awkward time, but was hoping to find you at home. He says the child is at school now, and she's of the right age: with your permission, he would be glad to see her at catechism next Saturday."

"There's no question of that," my mother cuts in sharply, staring down at some point on the tablecloth.

Five

Shortly after the beginning of the school term, there was a parents' meeting.

"There should be a law about these things, for goodness' sake. You can't put children in these situations."

"And what about ourselves? It's all so embarrassing. The very fact of having to speak of it . . ."

"My daughter's been having nightmares since the beginning of term."

"And my little girl – she wouldn't want me to tell you, but she's started wetting the bed again."

"And then, where have they kept her until now? Let her stay there! Her father has money enough to send her to school anywhere he likes!"

"Quiet, please!" Miss Albertina says.

"We're not in class now, Miss. You're not the boss now. We have a situation here – a problem to solve."

"But there is no problem at all," Miss Albertina says. "The children . . ."

"The children don't say anything to you! You have the knife by the handle in class every morning!"

"Will you be quiet! It's not that, Miss Albertina. We know what an exceptionally good teacher you are, and that you'll do everything you can. The point is . . . that child."

"Is she even normal?"

"I'm told she is, actually, and that she knows a lot."

"Oh she does, *I'm sure* – like a parrot."

"That's right, a parrot."

"Well, that's going a little too far, don't you think? It's all so embarrassing."

"She can't stay in a normal class. There are special schools for these cases. Her father is hardly short of money."

"But she is not some *case*," Miss Albertina says. "If you will just let me . . ."

"You have to tell it like it is – and stop beating about the bush."

"Don't say that, that's not right. Miss Albertina, we know how marvellously good you are, and that's why we want to talk to you before going ahead . . . I mean, the point is . . ."

"Going ahead with what, for heaven's sake? What is it you have in mind?" the teacher says abruptly.

"Going ahead, yes. There are lawyers among us and there are things that can be done."

"But she's the sweetest child. She was just unlucky. She's very bright – she plays the piano," Miss Albertina says hastily.

"Oh she does, *I'm sure* – some monkeys can play piano too. You can't deny the facts, Miss Albertina."

"The fact is, she even smells."

"That's quite enough!" the teacher says, unable to contain her exploding anger.

"*We'll* say what's enough here. This was done wrongly from the word go. We should have been warned of her coming. As parents, we should have been asked to give our opinion."

"I haven't seen her, but my daughter says she's a real monster."

"And then, can you imagine the school photographs?"

"That's right – the photos!"

"But that's not the point, I keep telling you! The point is, *she* can't be happy in a normal class, and Miss Albertina, who is so good, knows that very well."

"We must have the courage to do what's right. After all there are special schools where she could find friends of her own kind."

"That's right. My daughter says she never speaks to anyone."

"She never speaks because none of the other children will say a word to her. That's what they must learn," Miss Albertina says.

"They have to feel secure when they come to school, that's what! There's specially trained staff for people like that!"

"That's right. Of course we know these monsters exist, but that's no reason why we should . . ."

"What's monstrous is what I'm having to hear in this room," Miss Albertina says, raising her voice. But she is not accustomed to that, so her words come out in a screech: "I was tricked into coming here this evening. I would never, ever have come if I'd known. And if one single word of this loathsome meeting ever leaves the room, if the child or her parents are ever told about it, I – I will do something awful. I know things about every single person in this room. The hypocrisy caked all over your tongues and hearts – now that's what's monstrous."

"And then?" I ask Lucilla.

"Then she stormed out like one-pos-ses-sed, and I wasn't quick enough to move away from behind the door, so it got me – right here," she says, pointing to a raised purple bruise on her temple. "Then she asked me where Mamma was and I told her she hadn't been invited – imagine. But I found out and went along."

"What did she say?"

"Nothing. She made me swear I wouldn't tell you a-sin-gle-word about it."

Six

In my memory, the time I spent at primary school is like one of those toys resting on spirals of tightly coiled springs: they are harmless as long as they stay in their wooden boxes, but will scar you full in the face if you happen to open them carelessly.

Firmly sat on the lid was Miss Albertina, who carefully controlled any opening of the box, and whose presence kept my first steps into the world from causing me any hurt.

I made no friends at all apart from Lucilla, but equally I had no enemies to guard against.

In this too I was much helped by Lucilla, because the other schoolchildren tended to take us together, sharing out between us, and thus somewhat allaying, any surprise, curiosity or aversion they might have felt.

Seven

"We all knew it would end this way," Aunt Erminia is saying furiously.

She is sitting in one of the little armchairs in the hall. She must have stayed with us overnight: she was wearing sleek, dark green satin pyjamas that looked like an evening suit.

A noise had startled me out of sleep. From my bed I could hear the sound of steps, a sound much louder than all of us in the house would be able to make. So I got up. I found all the lights switched on. I walked across the empty rooms following the sound of the many voices, most of them absurdly unfamiliar. I stopped on the landing, wondering whether I should go downstairs. I feared the expression on the face of anyone that might see me for the first time, unless I could hold on tight to Maddalena's hand. After Aunt Erminia's, I can hear my father's quiet voice.

"She slept alone in the room at the back because she had problems with insomnia," he is saying. "She had been suffering from . . . from depression." I can hear that word taking its toll of sorrow on him. "For ten years."

With my head between the slender stone columns of the staircase, I could see my father standing in the hall in his blue dressing gown and slippers. He was speaking to a woman in uniform while Maddalena, badly slumped on the little armchair by the door, wept with her head in her hands as she answered questions from other persons, also in uniform.

"Was she receiving any medical care?" the policewoman asks.

"She was in my care," my father says. His arms are hanging along his body in a position that makes him look unnatural. "She would not accept any visits or doctors from outside. She was always . . . calm."

"You do realise we will need an autopsy," the policewoman is saying.

"Yes, I do," he says.

Then he seems to feel my eyes on him and turns around.

"Rebecca . . ."

"Papa . . ."

Perhaps he came up to me, or perhaps I went to him – but when he spoke again, I was holding on to him, my arms tight around his neck.

"Mamma . . . she fell into the river last night. She leant over the little balcony to see the lights of Monte Berico, as she sometimes did, and she slipped into the black water."

"Yes," the policewoman is saying as she strokes my head, her fingertips barely touching my hair. "She slipped, and the water was very cold last night."

"Where is she?" I say, my question falling into the silence that seems to have saturated the hall at once. "Where is she now?"

"She is gone for ever," my father says quietly.

I cannot trace the sequence of facts. I am not sure whether it was then that I began to dream of my mother, in her usual black dress, descending from heaven to my little balcony like a mourning Madonna and trying to speak to me but failing because I am totally deaf. Some other times I would dream of her as she fell into the river, perhaps crying out for help. Then she began to appear dressed in sky-blue, as I knew she had been on her wedding day. In the dream I would count the tiny white cornflowers around the neckline of her dress: one-two-three twelve on the right, one-two-three twelve on the left. I counted them again and again, looking sideways at her to check her mouth because I knew she was only waiting for a moment of silence from me so as to be able to speak, but instead of words her pale lips let fall a trickle of blood that crawled over her dress, marking the curve of her breast and hips and then all the way down to her left foot. A line that cut her in two, into before and after. At this point I would wake up screaming, and then start counting the ceiling beams, one-two-three twelve again, and the wooden planks laid across, one-two-three twenty-four.

In one other memory I am sitting at the piano, but not playing. I am bending double, my head resting against the keyboard and my arms clenched tight around myself, listening to my own heartbeat. Its pulse is so strong that it rhythmically moves one of the keys: do do do do. No no no no. The cold of the river comes through the wide-open windows and I let myself grow frozen: first my feet, then my legs, my head, my body, and last of all, my hands.

"May the Virgin of Monte Berico look upon us!" Maddalena says as she closes the windows.

Then she takes me in her arms, bunched up tight as I am, and sits in the little armchair next to the earthenware stove that spreads its dense heat around the room. She holds me tight, her breath through my hair, and as I relish the warmth of her body mixed with the heat from the stove, I say to myself: "I am ten years old."

Eight

Aside from Maddalena, I cannot remember anyone weeping when my mother died. Perhaps that was because there was no funeral, which is the proper occasion for weeping. And the reason why there was no funeral was simply that no-one knew how to take charge. When the priest appeared the next morning, bringing shy words of comfort, he did at some point mention that as far as he was concerned there was nothing to stop the funeral being celebrated in the beautiful church of Santa Caterina, at the foot of the Virgin of Monte Berico: "The Lord certainly knows how to comprehend her sorrow and our grieving," he said. But more than my father, it was Aunt Erminia who opposed the idea:

"My sister-in-law had lost her faith. It would be a real insult," she says to the priest, with a violence made all the stronger by the sharp nervous lines she is slashing in the air.

The priest is standing near the front door, and bows slightly to all of us:

"Grief is very powerful, and can push us to go where we truly do not want to go."

"You are all past masters in the grim art of assuming, without knowing and without listening, where people want to go and what they really want to do . . . My sister-in-law had wanted to die since . . . for years." She stops short, looking at me as if something is suddenly bothering her.

"And last night she made it," she says in the end, so softly that had the silence not been complete her words would have been lost in the rustle of the curtains on the landing.

I knew then that my mother had taken her own life, and some obscure shame whose origin I could not fathom made me lower my eyes – but no-one had any place for me in the desert of their thoughts. Only the priest, with an unpractised gesture, strokes my head:

"Nobody knows, even when they think they do. 'Right' and 'wrong' are words made to put good people on the cross."

"I think we are . . . inadequate for a funeral," my father says, preventing some terrible words that Aunt Erminia seems ready to utter. "But thank you, from all of us."

Nine

During the following days, Maddalena prepared me for all the visits we were meant to receive. She roamed around the house, blowing her nose into a huge handkerchief of finest muslin and trailing a wake of tears along the corridors and over the armchairs that she would move a few inches and then replace, without any conviction or necessity.

At regular intervals she turns abruptly towards me:

"You poor, poor child," she says as she crushes me in an embrace. "Poor child. We should have done something. But no, all quiet, always quiet, out of respect for the young Signora. Sooner or later she will get better, your father used to say. We mustn't force her. And this is the result. Truth was, it was easier for everyone that way. The young Signora out for the count and Madama Erminia holding court in her brother's house. And now, you'll see, she'll be moving in. But I'll take care of you, rest assured. No-one will send me away from here without you."

She ironed a pretty dress, electric blue with a white collar, that had been bought for me to wear at school parties and had remained in its box, and retrieved her many mourning clothes. She baked lemon and vanilla biscuits that filled the rooms with their heart-breaking aroma. She swept and dusted more than she usually did, because it was the right thing to do, she said, and because it kept her busy – and kept me busy.

Papa and Aunt Erminia had disappeared, wrapped up in all

the bureaucratic paperwork that follows a violent death – or so Maddalena said, over and over again, as if to convince herself. Nor did I dare ask about their very unusual absence. During those days I did not go to school, I did not know whether it was proper or not to play music, I did not have the courage to go near the piano.

On the third day, it became clear that we would receive no visits. The telephone also remained unaccountably silent: not one of my father's patients, not even Lucilla ever called.

"It's just not possible," Maddalena says over lunch, her tension exploding. It is Sunday and we are alone in the house. It is raining outside, and traffic noises are muted.

"Not possible."

She wipes her tears and says to me firmly: "You eat your *tiramisù*. I'll be back in a moment."

She was back an hour later, out of breath with haste, but even more so with outrage.

"Madama Erminia has told everyone that we wanted no visits. It seems she's had it printed in the newspaper as well. She just about stopped short of sticking posters all over town – just about!"

She was furious, and wept more than usual. She sensed how those missed visits were another wound for me, how in that way I was once again excluded.

"And then play, my child. You play! Save yourself!" She takes my hands in hers, delicately, as if she were praying: "You have life in your hands. Let us thank the Virgin and the Christ Child!"

She carries me upstairs, sits me at the piano and says:

"Play something that'll make us cry all of our tears, and let's be done with it!"

She let herself fall into the little white armchair in which my father used to sit in the evening, and sat listening, bolt upright, still wearing her jacket and hat. I chose a sad *siciliana* and played it with the anxious relief of one who can finally breathe again after risking suffocation.

And in the end someone did ring our doorbell – the next day, a few minutes before five. Maddalena and I went to open at the same moment, and found ourselves facing Miss Albertina. She was holding by the hand an extraordinarily dressed-up Lucilla.

"God bless you!" Maddalena says forcefully, taking hold of Miss Albertina's hand and sweeping her inside together with Lucilla. "God bless you both! We are just having tea. Will you join us?"

"With pleasure, thank you," Miss Albertina says, her hair bobbing up and down.

Lucilla links her arm through mine, and lingering a few steps behind Maddalena and Miss Albertina as we make our way upstairs she whispers:

"It was me who told my aunt that you'd cer-tain-ly be at home for your five o'clock tea! At school we had some surprises ready for you, some poems and letters to bring you: my aunt got us to make them. But then Murari, the son of the newspaper director, said your Aunt Erminia had spoken to the journalist who wrote the article about your mother, and dic-ta-ted to her that there were to be ab-so-lu-tely no visits. None-at-all. To respect your grieving, you understand? Then we thought we would give you all these things when you came back to school. But noth-ing-do-ing. No sign of you. So then I said to Aunt Albertina: 'We're going!' It's me who solves the problems in our house, as my Mamma always says. And here we are. How are you? Lovely dress. I've dressed up too. My Mamma wanted to come as well, but Aunt Albertina said no, it would feel like an in-va-sion. Everyone's thinking strange things about all this because . . ."

"What?" I say, interrupting her as I stop dead on the stairs.

"I real-ly-should-not tell you this. I've prom-ised. But they say that your father is finally free from a night-mare. That a handsome young man like him could ab-so-lu-tely not live like that, no way."

"Like what?"

"Like a gelding, they say."

"A gelding?"

"Someone who never makes love. You understand? A monk. Because clearly she never did, even though many say he must surely have found ways to con-sole-him-self."

"Who says that? How . . .?" I realise I do not even know what questions to ask.

"Where is your father now?"

"I don't know."

"And your Aunt Erminia?"

"I don't know. They are very busy with all the paperwork."

"All day long? They're who knows where, waiting for calm-on-the-troubled-waters."

"What waters?"

"Did you hear her fall?" she asks, very softly so as not to be overheard. "And why was your Aunt Erminia at the house that night?"

I can see myself standing next to the little table in the salon, where Maddalena is placing the teapot and cups, and suddenly feeling as if the floor were the black surface of the Retrone washing under my blue shoes, the silver buckle sinking fast out of sight and taking me along on its downward plunge.

"Help!" I call out, reaching out and catching hold of Miss Albertina.

"Holy Virgin of Monte Berico, she's dying!" Maddalena shrieks. And she lies me down on the floor that once again is solid as it should be.

"Rebecca is coming back to school tomorrow," I can hear Miss Albertina say. "Let her father know. If I don't see her, I shall call the police. She cannot be left locked up in here."

"She will come, rest assured," Maddalena says determinedly. "And if you do write a report for the social services, I shall sign it too."

An astonishing alliance was thus forged by chance on that day, one that would play a decisive role in my future. That threat of a report, something too frightening for me to ask about, was hardly ever voiced but only half mentioned in a whisper, one single time, in my father's presence. It was Maddalena who did it one day, after some disagreement of which I had not been aware. She did it casually, with her back to him, as she washed something in the sink with exaggerated care. Yet from that moment, that threat took up silent residence in each corner of our house, ready to be floated fearlessly whenever a decision needed to be made. A powerful weapon in Maddalena's hands.

When Maddalena came to collect me from school, she would often stop to talk with Miss Albertina. Normally I could not hear what they were saying, and whenever I did, it was usually some harmless exchange of information about homework or the weather. Yet I knew that their curious alliance was about me, that they were keeping watch over something, without perhaps even knowing exactly what it was.

A few days later Papa returned home, without any explanations, and resumed work between his clinic and the hospital. Aunt Erminia also reappeared: she arrived one evening at suppertime, tanned and perfumed, more beautiful than I had ever seen her. She spoke little, and mostly about music, the *conservatoire* and her untalented pupils. Throughout the evening, each one of her remarks went unanswered. When she left, we did not feel in the least reassured.

Ten

Aunt Erminia moved in with us a few weeks after Mamma's death. She came trailing a swarm of perfumes and colours that left their wake in each room of the house. I knew the one she loved best, a brand new, luscious fragrance dedicated to Chopin by a French *parfumier*: a mix of jasmine, orange and rose fading into Oriental notes of ylang-ylang and sandalwood. It had the texture, magical to my eyes, of an invisible veil that spread around her with every step she took, when she played, when she turned to smile at us, when she said goodbye. But the bathroom also overflowed with the mix of scents from her bodycare cosmetics: the passionflower cream she spread on her legs, the almond oil she used as an overnight mask for her hair. Often in the evening she would take me into the bathroom with her and talk to me as she tended to that body brimming with beauty. She would tell me about her pupils. Some were at school with me, and I liked to hear that they were much less gifted than I was, that they had made a huge mess of their end of year show, that they were unable to get going again if they missed a beat. I was still dreaming of the *conservatoire*, but Aunt Erminia would not budge on that.

"It's as your father wants: not until you've finished primary school," she says firmly. "And anyway, the less you mix with that flock of trained geese who only get in because their parents push and kick them, the better chance you'll have to develop your own style. Anyone can play well, but what matters is finding your own music inside."

"Like Bach, you mean?" I needle her because the pitch of her fury gives me a shiver of pleasure.

"Bach! A stiff-necked Protestant bigot, prolific as a battery rabbit, who was lucky enough to catch one dead-boring refrain floating around in the *Zeitgeist* and then sanctified it by sticking it full of praise the Lord in the highest, amen!" she declaims, drawing a wide and final sign of the cross in the air.

"What about Wagner?"

"Music for the deaf. Hit the vibrations hard enough, and even the deaf will get the gist."

"What about Mozart?"

"An incontinent two-timer with delusions of erotic omnipotence. Wrote music for the serial seduction of schoolgirls. Save the 'Requiem': the 'Requiem' alone is worth the whole insipid life of that powdered coxcomb – the rest can be forgiven. Perhaps, right on life's threshold, the God of secret designs gave him a glimpse of the abyss he was about to plummet into and allowed him to transcribe one small glimmer for our warning and edification."

And she stretches her arms in front of her to protect me from that wrathful gaze whose mere mention seems to scare her too.

I adored my evening conversations with Aunt Erminia: the vertigo I derived from familiarity with that perfect body held me high in a sort of free zone where everything was permitted – even forgetting one's own ugliness.

"We must renew the whole house," she says over breakfast one morning, her glossy black hair dark as a moonless night against her bright green dressing gown.

"Things carry the stories they have lived through, and we need space for new stories in here."

No-one answers. Maddalena places the bread basket on the sideboard with a heavy thump as she stares at my father from behind Aunt Erminia's back.

"We could start with the colours: they're too faint. It feels like living inside a box of stale candy. In the long run, colours like these make people weak," she says undaunted, her hands miming a jittery shake.

What happened to me at that moment was like what we sometimes live through in nightmares, when we want to speak and are unable to: the mouth gapes in the painful physical effort to utter a sound, the eyes open wide as if staring straight at some terrible danger. But I could say nothing, and felt myself suffocating from a violent contraction inside my throat.

All I wanted was to speak and say that those colours were my colours too, that nothing in the world would induce me to part with the sunny yellow of my bedroom or the sky-blue of the curtains in the salon, the walls in the hall, the kitchen fixtures. Those colours belonged to me more than my name that no-one ever used: they wrapped themselves around me, enfolding me whenever I moved from one room to the other or fell asleep at night. They were the colours my mother had chosen and not changed after my birth. They were the thread of continuity leading back to her own dreams, they were what she was before I was born. But these were not conscious thoughts for me – only a hard knot stopping my breath.

"I don't think so," my father says very quietly. "I really don't think so," he repeats in a louder voice as Aunt Erminia stalks out, shaking her shoulders as if to shrug off some noisome weight.

After Aunt Erminia stopped giving me piano lessons, I began to compose my own music. I only did it when she was not around, and often in the presence of Lucilla, who came to visit in the afternoon and knew how to bring out my playful mood.

"Imagine you're at the Teatro Olimpico," she says, intoning her words like a hypnotist. "That's right. Or better still, at the Arena, in Verona. Can you imagine?"

"I don't know, I've never been there."

"Oh my God, then you must-ab-so-lu-tely come with us next time we go. I've been a-ny-num-ber of times! My mother takes me every summer, for the opera, you know, the shows – and also if she's got something serious to make up for. Anyway, imagine an amphitheatre like the Romans': it's e-nor-mous, very dark and full-of-people."

She gets up and turns off the light.

"And you are playing. No-one can see you and you're playing playing playing something no-one's ever heard before and everyone's saying 'Who is she? Does anyone know her? She's a mir-acle-of-na-ture!' And they listen, they listen in silence . . ."

And wrapped in the sweet darkness veined with pale blue I would play, I would make stately *adagios* out of the slow rhythm of the timeless days that had followed my mother's death, as the black water that had lured her turned into an obsessive theme set again and again in variations of ever-increasing speed and intricacy chasing into each other without respite.

"What's this one?" Lucilla says.

"It's the water of the Retrone," I say as I ripple through an *arpeggio*, a water sound starting on a high note and falling deeper and deeper down to the low notes on the keyboard until it turns into a graceless roar.

"It's scary."

"No it isn't – if it's music it isn't."

"Now play the rain."

The rain too starts sharp and clear and then turns into a storm that tears things down.

"Do the storm that ends and the blue sky coming back."

But she did not like my blue-sky music. It came out like variations on Pachelbel: changeable enough, but still giving away the main theme. Reassuring, yes – but hardly new.

"I want a music that doesn't remember sorrow," she suddenly says one day.

I remain motionless, my fingers touching the edge of the keyboard as I struggle to find the notes.

It is dark around me, but it's not Lucilla's doing. I realise it is almost evening.

"No, I can't."

Eleven

Very young girls think they can become anything: princesses, doctors, teachers, actresses. An ugly child knows she will always be just ugly.

An ugly child has no plans for the future. She fears it and does not look forward to it, because she cannot imagine it to be any better than the present. She listens to the plans made by other girls and knows, has always known, that they do not concern her. So she thinks she feels no sorrow if she happens to guess the wishes of those describing their own future as models, singers, airline stewardesses, ballerinas, barristers, physicians, office workers or professors. That is the other girls' world. At times she catches herself thinking there might be work that can be done while remaining hidden, staying indoors, in the dark – but she does not know about that and is scared to ask.

Just like there is no work, so there is no partner in her future: she knows that no-one will ever feel for her anything more benevolent than pity.

An ugly child cannot even love the past, since it does not carry any happy memories. In fact she wishes with all her strength that she could erase bad memories, but she cannot, because even the hurt of being offended is life, and thus preferable to the nothingness of indifference.

An ugly child can of course have dreams, but each awakening causes her to sink deeper and deeper down, and so she soon loses that art.

Twelve

The first summer after my mother's death loomed ahead, terrifying. The winter had passed among lessons, homework, the visits from Lucilla, the evenings with Aunt Erminia. But with the end of the school term in June, I was overcome with emptiness. On the last day I felt more unhappy than I ever had before. The other children talked about the holidays they would take during those months, that time of passage between primary and secondary school, while for the first time I became aware of being different in ways other than those determined by my looks. My mother's presence had filled my days in spite of everything. She was enough for me. If she was in the little drawing-room, I would incessantly walk up and down the stairs, on the slightest pretext, or sometimes on no pretext at all, so as to make sure, glancing sideways into the room, that she was there. I did not really look at her: I was content with that dark shadow in the corner of my eye, the black spot that spoke her presence.

If she was in her bedroom, I would make sure the doors were open, and play my piano. My mother always left her bedroom door ajar, and deep down I know I was hoping she did that for me. And then sometimes I would stop playing to slide silently along the corridor leading to the bedrooms, and quickly pass in front of hers. She always faced away from the door, and often sat at the little dressing table that she used as a desk, without ever seeming to notice me.

But with her death my days became empty. And with the end of the school year they turned into gaping chasms. Aunt Erminia told us of an important concert in Milan and said she would not be back for several days. After the tragedy she had stopped teaching me, and I had not dared ask her about it. I would play, but without the audience – voiceless and inexpressive, perhaps even deaf but an audience nonetheless – that my mother's presence had been.

In the evening, only Maddalena would sometimes sit and listen to me, although music made her weep even more than usual. She would listen and sigh, letting large teardrops fall heavily onto her blue apron.

"I am Maestro Aliberto De Lellis – I have come for the piano lesson."

A tall man, perhaps no longer young, with large and inquisitive clear eyes, is bowing towards some midpoint between me and Maddalena. He is dressed in an oversized white suit and, despite the heat that makes the air shimmer over the tarmac, he is wearing a tie.

His age seems to vary according to the point on which I rest my gaze: his clothes push him towards the threshold of middle age, his fair hair and relaxed smile make him look much younger. We are standing in front of the open front door, not knowing how to deal with this apparition and its unlikely name.

"Welcome," Maddalena says at last – but she cannot quite decide to let him in, as if she did not fully trust him. "Did Madama Erminia send you? I'm so sorry, perhaps she forgot to mention to us . . ."

71

"Oh, no wonder, the poor darling. Ever since she stopped teaching she . . ."

"Stopped teaching?" we both say, interrupting him at the same time.

"Yes. She gave notice at the *conservatoire* after . . . after the events . . . the event . . ." he says, looking at me.

"But she's always talking about her pupils . . ." I start, then stop short, realising I have said something wrong.

"It really has been awful," Maddalena says with finality, moving aside a little, but not far enough to let the Maestro in.

"As I have learnt from Erminia herself, having met her by chance in Venice . . ."

"Venice," Maddalena repeats.

"That's right – having learnt that she feels, how shall I put it . . . guilty, no longer being able to teach this outstanding niece of hers," and he holds out his hand as if wanting to shake mine, but thinks better of it, "about whom she has told me so much at the *conservatoire* – I am one of her colleagues, I should have told you – I have offered to help. I have a love of talents that are . . . special," he says, and bows again, towards me this time.

His voice is as hesitant as his movements, but he does not seem intimidated by not being expected.

"We are having tea. Would you like a cup?" Maddalena says: she has decided to trust him.

"Yes, please."

And suddenly, as we walk upstairs, he takes my hand. With an abrupt gesture, a pull sharp as a break-off shot on green baize, he grips my hand in his. The unexpected promise of a lasting presence. He was the first person to ever take my hand of his own accord, rather than as prescribed by good manners or social role. The shock I felt overcame any possible reaction on my part: I gave my hand up to him, abandoned it to his, which was cool as a child's, soft as a pianist's.

It was he who filled my days during that summer. He was a calm man with elegant manners, and the emotions that somehow passed between us helped me to temper the passion of the music I played with him.

He steered me out of Aunt Erminia's riotous romanticism and taught me to love the geometric harmonies in Bach, the enigmatic quality of Russian composers, the tightly coiled, unreleased vitality of Vivaldi, whose Bach transcriptions for the clavichord he would happily play for me. He would express the pleasure of teaching me what he knew in the form of old-fashioned compliments:

"Oh-oh! Despite your truly young age, Signorina, you have executed this *pavane* in impeccable style!"

I found those compliments charming. And I loved the way he would make me repeat any difficult passages, patiently, without ever seeming to grow tired. After the storm that was Aunt Erminia, the measured flowing of his hands over the keys was healing the tension that inhabited me.

Maddalena inflicted many long pauses and many cups of tea on him before finally finding the courage to ask. Reticent, he would change the subject with delicate courtesy, congratulate her on the ever-varied flavours of her biscuits, enquire about my love of vanilla. But our opportunity to learn about unknown aspects of Aunt Erminia did come in the end.

"Does she have any men then?" Maddalena says one afternoon, blurting out the words with the pinch of bad grace that always accompanies indiscreet questions.

"Well . . . not as far as one would know . . . or say," the Maestro says cautiously. "Certainly, many have . . . tried. To go out with her, I mean. To pay her a compliment to . . . test the ground, so to speak. But they had no luck – none at all. She just laughs and runs away."

"That's not normal, is it," Maddalena says sternly. "It's one thing to take vows, and then it's fair enough. But otherwise . . . besides, she's always so provocative."

"She is," the Maestro says, agreeing in spite of himself.

"A *bronsa cuerta*. Could she be a *bronsa cuerta*?"

"I'm not sure I understand," De Lellis says guardedly.

"A smothered ember: looks like a saintly little virgin but is actually a man eater," Maddalena says with a dose of brutality.

"I wouldn't know," the Maestro says conclusively.

Aunt Erminia seldom came home that summer. After the lie she had told us about her concert in Milan, she gave us to understand that she was going on holiday, but never sent a postcard from anywhere. Nor did anyone ever ask her any questions. Our evening conversations at her bath time had grown much less frequent, and she never enquired about the Maestro or complained about the new music that she sometimes happened to hear me play. September would bring my audition at the *conservatoire* – so she told me many times, as if to remind herself. I certainly could never have forgotten about it.

"Do people talk about Madama Erminia?"

At the question, a slight jolt runs through the Maestro's hand, and he spills a few drops of dark tea on the spotless white lace of the tablecloth.

"No. I – I wouldn't know."

"Would you tell me if you did?"

"I . . . no, I don't think I would."

"Who could tell me then?"

"It is not always good to know."

Thirteen

"Quiet – Mamma's asleep," Lucilla says as I walk into her flat on a sultry afternoon that summer.

"Is she ill?"

There is a silence that feels unnatural in Lucilla's home.

"No. She had a-wild-night."

"A wild night?"

"A-hot-night."

"A hot night?"

"Well . . . with a man, I mean."

"Which man? Is your father back?"

"What a shock-ing-i-dea. Rath-er-dead than with him, even if he did come back. No – with a painter, in fact."

"With a painter. And why?"

"Because ev-ery-one has a man at the right age and with the right-oc-ca-sion. But don't-say-a-word," she says with her finger across her lips and her face nearly touching mine. "I don't know any-thing-at-all, officially."

Later her mother got up, switched the radio on in the kitchen, made a chocolate soufflé.

"There's pudding for you two," she says, walking into Lucilla's room as we sit listening to music. "Vanilla chocolate – just as you like it, Rebecca."

I look intently first at her mild round face and then at the sweeping curves of her body, huge but supple as it moves in her golden yellow summer dress: I am searching for the secret of that night I cannot imagine. Then I think, she makes cakes that are like her.

I went back home shortly before supper. There was no-one in. Maddalena was away on some errands I knew nothing about, my father at his clinic or at the hospital as usual.

The silence was plunged in the cool penumbra of the shuttered balconies and drawn curtains. I sat in the little armchair next to the front door. No-one broke the silence until Maddalena's return.

Suddenly I think that we all have the life we deserve, but I do not know why.

Fourteen

That summer, after the end of the school term, my father also disappeared. He would nearly always come home late in the evening, long after supper, when he was sure that I had already started on my unfailing bedtime rituals. He knew that Maddalena kept watch over this orderly sequence of actions as if it were a sacred office, something meant to bring the day to a close with rigour and grace, a reference point over which life's chaos was utterly powerless. And so he would greet me briefly, standing on the threshold of my bedroom, not coming in, not approaching, not looking into my eyes. Sometimes he happened to be home for supper, and then we would eat in a silence even deeper than when my mother had been alive. Only when Aunt Erminia came did our suppers become slightly livelier, turning into the self-conscious and overexcited show of a highly strung actor.

Maddalena and I had learnt from Maestro De Lellis about her roaming from one city to the other, and would let her tell us all about her gruelling orchestra rehearsals without questioning or contradicting her. I have no idea of what my father might have known, but on those evenings he seemed to fear any silent pause, and so filled the moments in which Aunt Erminia was eating with anxious and minutely detailed questions about the scores, the music stands, the acoustics in the auditorium, the colour of the seats, the behaviour of the orchestral musicians.

He spent that whole summer at work. Little by little, his patients began to call him again, seeking respite from the many fears attendant on pregnancy and birth. By now I too was answering the telephone, and had learnt how to speak to those ladies if my father was away: I knew how to reassure them, telling them that he was bound to be at the hospital, that they would find him there, and if not to call again and we would look for him. I loved that grown-up role: it allowed me to exist while avoiding any exposure to the world's shock, disgust, pain and superstitious reactions. For the first time I found a normal dimension that not even music had given me, because even when I was playing my body would offend the sight of any listener. To be voice and voice alone gave me a whole new and unsuspected range of possibilities: I could be gentle or professional, brisk or relaxed, tentative or self-assured. I felt free to ask, to reply, to play for time. I could try out all the variations, searching for my own style in the voice, since I was not allowed to have one in life.

My voice would obey me exactly as my hands did when I played. It grew deep, resonant, rolling its r's like my father's or quivering with anger or emotion like Maddalena's.

I knew most of my father's patients, and could remember their names, their pathologies and their personalities, because of the way he had described them, with deep humanity and gentleness, to my mother every evening. She might not have been listening, withdrawing perhaps behind the impossibly high, icy walls of her fortress, and the words of that man who was so full of life and sorrow might not even have reached her ears as a sort of tiresome buzzing. But those ladies mattered to me, they who entrusted my father with their hopes and their pain and whom he would shelter

79

and understand, coming to know them in the end better than they knew themselves, like a musician who, free from all envy and disrespect, rewrites with each concert a truth that the composer is not aware of having committed to the score.

I could imagine them one by one, their bellies swollen with children, or cancers, or fears and desires. One very young, small woman, a chatty, tiny pixie with curly blonde hair who wore flat golden pumps even in winter, had been expecting twins who must have been born that March. I had lost contact with her: my mother's death had interrupted Papa's evening updates. She was back now, with a voice that was fully her own, shrill, precise, imperious with urgency, because of a worrying complaint, described vaguely at first, and then more and more specifically as she responded to my calm voice: a pain between her navel and pubic area.

"Does it seem to be progressively worsening?" I say. I love these terms pregnant with complicity.

"Yes, it does – it's worsening by the day, by the hour even. It's unbearable. I need the doctor, now."

I make a quick, prudent assessment, then say:

"Perhaps some exertion? Did you have a Caesarean?" I can remember things.

"Yes, I did. And I did clear out one of my bookcases, and then shifted some boxes of books. But the Caesarean was five months ago . . ."

"Perhaps you had several stitches, the tissue is still fragile." I can remember exactly: a haemorrhage, a long long railway line of tiny stitches, as Papa had told Mamma one evening.

"That's true," she says with relief.

"I will pass your message on anyway, and we'll get back to you as soon as possible."

The new voices effortlessly matched the images that my father had conveyed of his patients, and gave fresh life to this world of ladies who surely did not know the person they were addressing on the telephone: I was extremely careful to modulate my very young voice, preserving intact the form of the play-acting that allowed me to move in my father's adult world. At first, if Maddalena was at home, I let her answer the telephone, only taking calls when she was out shopping: I would sink into the beautiful navy blue jacquard armchair in my father's study, with the nape of my neck over the edge of the back, one hand holding the receiver and the other relaxed on the armrest, and I would speak, listen, reassure, mentally take notes, extend polite greetings.

One day it happened: when Maddalena came back I was engaged in a call and could not alter my voice or the register of that conversation. I sensed her standing still on the stairs and listening, I imagined she might be uncertain as to whether to intervene or not. She did not say anything, and from then on I also took calls when she was at home. We never spoke of that between ourselves, nor with my father, who certainly must have understood what was happening very quickly, piecing together his patients' accounts with the messages I would leave as notes on his desk or telephone memos dictated to his secretary at the clinic.

Only when Lucilla was there would I keep away from the telephone: much as I adored her, I knew that no promise or solemn undertaking would ever rein in her powerful need to live by communicating all things to all people. One day I stopped taking calls, but by then I had discovered a way to be in the world, a possible existence. Beauty wants to be seen, but for me, the saving grace was invisibility.

Fifteen

Adolescence took my life by storm, ambushing it and then smashing it open with the wholesale, indifferent rage of a hurricane, without anyone noticing. By then I had already lost Lucilla – or so I thought at the time – and also Miss Albertina, who had been replaced by a cohort of ashen professors with voices that cracked like whips, who called their students by surname, mistook them for one another as if they were pawns on a chessboard, and in fact did move them like pawns around the classroom each time a buzz of chatter was deemed in any way subversive.

I had to cross a small part of the city to make my way to Contrà Riale: I would walk past the Retrone, then in Piazza Matteotti pass the snow-white columns of Palazzo Chiericati, walk up Corso Palladio as far as the austere Contrà Porte that held the most precious buildings in the city, and then down Contrà Riale, towards the "good school" of Vicenza. An ungainly grey building, it had a huge entry gate with peeling paint, but only a tiny door cut inside this gate would ever open for the children to walk in single file into a gloomy, dimly lit hall. Nothing in that building complied with any existing norm – indeed nothing was even simply normal. The stairs curled and coiled up three storeys with their high steps of polished and slippery marble worn down by the passing generations. Each year, as punctual as the autumn rain, some of the children would fall and fracture an arm, a kneecap, in one case even a vertebra. The rooms were too high, and there was no system capable of heating their stone floors, from which a bitter, paralysing cold rose all the way to our knees.

Maddalena had an apparently unwarranted aversion for that school, but had not stood against Aunt Erminia's wish – certainly not out of fear of her, but rather because of a sense of awe for what she, as a person of little formal education, felt was a high and sacred ideal to which one could sacrifice the wish for a healthier and better attended environment.

"Holy Virgin of Monte Berico! What happened to you?"

There is no hiding from Maddalena: she can hear the unusual hesitation with which I am opening our front door, the heavier thump of my school bag onto one of the little armchairs in the hall, the jittery, slow pace at which I am climbing up the stairs, leaning on my right foot as if it were a walking stick, my hand crawling up the banister and not finding a way to lift itself.

But there are no words to tell everything – not at that age. Sometimes one learns them later, when they have lost their smell, their colour, and above all their sorrow.

"The needle's eye" – that was the name I gave to that narrow fissure that swallowed me into its blackness each morning and then, once digested, vomited me out after the day's lessons.

To the very last day, I walked through the school gate exactly like the camel in the Gospel, constricting myself in the effort to shrink, grow thinner, disappear. I had not learnt the art of rebellion, and walked through the darkness of the hall in full knowledge of what lay in wait for me, without that knowledge ever diminishing the terror I felt. One cannot forestall the offence that drives a nail into the body and the spirit, piercing the spirit through the body.

The first to begin was the beadle, Albina. She was perched on a sort of huge wooden trestle at the bottom of the stairs so she could warn the children to take care while climbing up, "else you will slip on the steps and *breakyourneck*." She was tacitly exonerated from any type of work because of her excess fat. The trestle on which she was balanced like a medieval monk on the misericord of a choir stall had no back or armrests, so as to allow her hips to ooze out over the three sides and tumble down all around her into a flabbergasting heap, made even more monstrous by the enormous black smock that covered it.

Whenever I passed her, she took special care to avoid looking at me, and never spoke to me, but after I had climbed the first few steps, she would furtively cross herself, in a sort of pagan ritual of her own which would exorcise the evil that surely must emanate from a graceless, monstrous creature such as I.

Out of the corner of my eye, I could just about catch a glimpse of her hand lifting in a quick movement that would readily turn into a gesture of annoyance against some non-existing insect if I happened to slow down, giving her the impression that I might be turning around. But I never did.

And then there were the other children. I realise now this must be an inaccurate memory, because three years at school are a very long time for such a relentless exercise in sadism, but I cannot think of one friendly, polite or even neutral expression ever addressed to me by any of them. I think they must all have perceived me as a black hole in the continuity of the classroom space.

Yet they could see me very well indeed, since on the first day of school I had found the seats already allocated, and the white card with my name had been placed on the desk in the middle of the first row, right in front of the teacher's desk. And there it stayed, the only pawn to remain fixed, cemented, unmoved in its place for three years.

"The witchie. The ootlin. She's a craw-bogle." The few who can resort to the dialect spoken by their country grandparents bring out expressions that have not often been heard under the noble eaves of the time-honoured school of Contrà Riale.

"You suety, putrid little hair tuft." Some play with cultured alliterations.

"*Homuncula, foetidissima.*" Some with the Latin overheard from older siblings.

Their words came hissing, sharp as pins, or shouted, like spikes stabbing my back. I recognised their voices: like the blind, I got my bearings through sound in that universe teeming with treacherous life behind me, and more than the god Janus I knew the past and future of each one of them, because I could also hear the whispers addressed to a favourite friend, or the sighs they would keep to themselves.

No-one took the place of Miss Albertina in ensuring that the world in which I spent half of my days would retain some form of order. Anything could be said, anything could – and did – happen.

"Who can tell me where the Pamir range is? Does anyone remember the date of the Battle of Hastings? The name of the last Catholic king to rule over England? The symbol for carbon? The rules of badminton? How many miles of coastline does Italy have? How many does Sicily have? What about Veneto? When was the Republic of Venice founded?"

At school I did well out of desperation, so that I could impose some boundaries on chaos and somehow avoid being cut adrift and falling off the edge: the last mooring. If I know things nothing will go wrong, nothing bad will happen if every little piece of science and knowledge is in its proper place, with its own name and surname.

I was not really interested and would never show off, but only answered out of necessity, so as to stop up the holes into which I might have fallen. And also because, through my voice, I could feel that I existed.

On the other hand, and for the same reasons, my words went to swell the resentment that the other children felt against me.

They were not generally very gifted for school work. The girls might have been more diligent, or at least known how to look like they were, and if they were caught unprepared, they were ready to gracefully repeat that they had studied ever so much, but really, really did find the subject so hard to understand. The teachers would play the game and exhort them to try again – that paragraph was very, very easy after all. The boys would just not study, making a show of defiance. But like the girls, they were all somebody's children, and the teachers' subservience towards fathers, mothers, uncles, aunts or grandparents would take different forms, showing now as indulgence, now as debonair paternalism, and sometimes, with the weaker teachers, as downright fear.

This explains why no-one wanted to see or hear anything of what happened.

Some of the girls might have wanted to pass through the cone of shadow inside which I was moving. Sometimes I would catch a glance recognising me as a human being, a smile tinged with confusion, uncertainty, anxiety: shall I speak to her, what shall I say, what will the others say, no I shan't. And for my part I would not encourage anyone to approach in any way. Not out of choice – out of incapability.

I too was somebody's daughter, but my father was unpractised at the art of bestowing favours with the calculated precision that ensures one's position in a small-town world of privilege, the world that counts and shelters its own from offence. His was an extravagant, mindless generosity that prevented him from keeping count of who and how much, and even kept him safe from having to suffer gratitude.

"He's with the daughter of the newspaper lady of Piazza Matteotti – she had a crisis at seven o'clock. Perfectly capable of not coming back till the middle of the night. He's burning out like a stook of dried stubble left in the middle of an August field!"

A furious Aunt Erminia takes her seat in front of the asparagus mousse especially prepared for their birthday supper and starts noisily drumming her fingers on the table.

"She's very ill," Maddalena says as she serves the croutons. "She has cancer at the final stage, the poor young thing. He's been taking care of her ever since he found it in her breast. By now it has spread to her bones – she'll be gone in a breath leaving three little orphans, if the Virgin of Monte Berico doesn't look down in a hurry." And she wipes away her tears.

"The city is full of tragedies," Aunt Erminia shoots back furiously, thumping the table with her open hand. "Must my brother shoulder them all?"

But hers is not meanness, only something that Maddalena calls "the tantrums of Madama Erminia": summer lightning, excess energy, no storm afterwards. It is her need for perfection and her powerlessness in the face of a world that will not match it, that will allow evil, allow her twin brother to miss their birthday supper. It is also a kind of self-centredness that has the transparency and solidity of diamond carbon, so pure that it can make those around her blind to discriminating judgement. Those who damned themselves to grant her a favour, no matter how capricious, always felt as if they were receiving one from her.

My father could move around the city unfettered by gossip, and although he knew so much about everyone, since his patients would entrust him with their bodies and their sorrows as if he had been a confessor, the idea of cultivating a hierarchy in his relationships never even touched his mind.

That is why his name did not protect me and, afterwards, did not ensure that justice would be granted to me.

Sixteen

In the afternoon I would rush to the *conservatoire*, just a few steps
from home, at the Ponte degli Angeli. The *conservatoire* also had a
staircase, but this was a grand stairway of honour made of highly
polished marble, where one felt like dancing to the notes gliding
down in a dissonant tangle from the three storeys of music classrooms. I was unaware of that desire back then, but now I know
I felt it, because these days, each time I climb those stairs, un-
ravelling as I do so the merry riot of sounds coming from the
classrooms, recognising the Boccherini of a cello student, the
Vivaldi being practised on the flute or the Clementi of the first piano
grades, I find myself stepping more lightly, taken by a faraway
feeling, a childhood caress at once innocent and momentous.

"Does my young pupil have something of her own to propose
today?"

This was the greeting with which Maestro De Lellis, who had
wanted me as one of his pupils, always welcomed me.

I owed my admission to the *conservatoire* the previous autumn
to him. That is why Aunt Erminia was crying when she came out
of the audition room: it was the humiliation she suffered when
her opinion, her "furious striving", as she had called it when she
told me about it some time later, had not been enough.

"Maestro De Lellis stood up while everyone was shouting at
everyone else and no-one was listening to me, no-one at all – as if
I didn't exist. He waited for silence and then said that probably,

unless the merciful God of Christians gave proof of his existence in this life, you would never become a concert pianist, and unfortunately not a teacher either, since the world *merely deigns*, as he said, to celebrate appearance, ephemera, the rind, the disgusting grease paint of common decorum – those were his exact words, they sounded like they came straight from some Victorian preacher a hundred years ago. But that in your hands you possess the art of creation, the gift to call back to life, through music, the beauty that was denied to you. That we could but welcome and cultivate it, that we should thank the circumstances, or God if we are so inclined, for being given this opportunity. That he didn't know how, but there had to be a way in which this gift would do good to the human race."

Clearly I did not compose my own music at the same speed at which I would learn the pieces assigned by Maestro De Lellis, but whenever I did have something to propose our lessons would gain the intoxicating quality of a wild run through autumn mist. I felt the dangerous pleasure of letting myself go, the excitement of a child at play, the fear and yet the need to be daring, to listen, to counteract, to disagree. The grace of forgetting my cruel shape. Maestro De Lellis gave me space and guided me, and I was grateful to him for it. There was no offence, it was not about me, it was for music, for the piece that in the end would come out new, unlike anything that had existed before, created, or generated, by me.

"It would be . . . embarrassing, you understand – on stage, like that, with all the others. Embarrassing for her, above all. And for the *conservatoire* too, for the other children, and . . . the parents. But above all for her."

I do not know who is behind the classroom door, I cannot hear the reply given by Maestro De Lellis, who as ever is speaking in a quiet voice.

I turn back taking care not to be heard and walk very slowly down the marble stairway. I wait in the hall reading the concert notices, then go back upstairs.

"I won't play at the end of year recital," I say as I throw the door wide open.

"I understand . . . it is meant to be compulsory, but we can consider a few possibilities . . ." the Maestro says with a smile.

"No possibilities. I won't do it."

I had learnt my place. At school, in the morning, I could not escape: I would sit like a statue born from the clumsiness of an unskilled craftsman, hoping to blend in with the desks scarred by markings, the splintered chairs, the worn, crazed marble tiling of the floor, the walls tacky with yellowed old adhesive tape. At the *conservatoire* I was not the target of any offence – but that was also because I would not open out beyond the space assigned to my presence, which was the classroom of Maestro De Lellis.

I knew nothing about him: since no-one would speak to me, I was party to no gossip or sharing of secrets. That was another reason why I missed Lucilla.

"He's not married. He lives nearby, that's why he walks to our house and also to the *conservatoire*. On Viale Dante, in a villa along the main road to Monte Berico. His mother, the old Signora, is a little cracked. She must be tinder-dry by now. His grandparents were from one of the city's good families. Notaries. His grand-father died the day after his wife was buried."

A tear gushes away from Maddalena, who is answering my questions about the Maestro.

"How did he die?"

"He . . . he committed suicide. For love. For love of his wife. Very romantic, they said. And since he was who he was, they even gave him the blessing before taking him to the cemetery. Not to church, because that was too big a sin for those times, but the priest did take him to the cemetery and they put him in the family vault. It was his daughter found him – the old Signora. She didn't go to the funeral: they were not on very good terms. May the Virgin forgive her – but she did have her reasons." She is wiping her tears as they fall on the freshly ironed whites.

"What reasons?"

"Well – gentlemen and ladies prize their good name more than life itself. And I've said too much already."

"And you – did you forgive the Virgin?"

"What are you saying?"

"For making your children die, I mean. And your husband too."

After the hours spent at school in the morning, my control slackens. I build up some credit that settles for a few hours the debt I contracted at birth because of my terrifying ugliness.

"Don't go saying these awful things, for the love of the Holy Virgin. She didn't make them, they just died. Life is mystery. Is it blasphemy they teach you, in Contrà Riale?"

She did not know how close she was to the truth.

During that first winter of secondary school, after lunch, when the cold kept old people resting in their houses, whenever I had

93

no classes at the *conservatoire* I would go out, well wrapped in my blue coat, with my blue hat and blue scarf to protect myself from drivers' eyes. Walking along Via Giuriolo and part of Viale Regina Margherita, I would climb the flight of steps leading up to Monte Berico to then go down towards Viale Dante and reach the house of Maestro De Lellis. I could have taken the lower route, following the road from its beginning: that would have made the climb easier, but I preferred the flight of steps that reminded me of my evening jaunts with Aunt Erminia. I had kept the habit of running as I climbed, savouring the pleasure of exhaustion that emptied me of all the cares from my mornings at school. I would not stop in front of the locked gate, but walk past quickly, with hardly a glance, and then two houses down I would cross the road and retrace my steps, passing the house gate again and glancing once more through its bars. At the Piazzale del Cristo, where the row of porticos leading Sunday pilgrims to the Basilica takes a right turn, I would sit for a few minutes on the bench in front of the Carmelites' monastery, and then, still running, make my way down and back home. A little ritual after which I would start playing, listening to music and doing homework.

In this way I had built a fairly clear picture of my teacher's house. It was a small two-storey villa, white and well kept. Unlike the neighbouring ones, it had no balconies but large windows only screened by pastel curtains, often open to show glass chandeliers. There was a huge one on the upper floor, its crystal drops glimmering with bright light and moving as if swaying in a gentle breeze whose origin I could not imagine. And always, each day, the sound of a piano could be heard: someone was listening to

94

piano music, without interruption, every afternoon. Or playing it. At least so I thought, sometimes.

"It's wrong to peek into people's houses," Maddalena says sternly when I tell her about my excursions. But then her curiosity prevails:

"And what is the park like?"

Its size was that of a garden, but it had trees so tall in fact as to recall the great expanse of Parco Querini, near the new city hospital. There was a cedar whose main trunk opened out into three sturdy arms like a candlestick, stretching high over the gate towards the roof of the house. Once, during that time, I dreamt I was asleep in the almost level space at the base of the three arms, a space protected by that mighty natural trinity that seemed to be offering me up like a gift to heaven. Or protecting me from heaven, perhaps.

Behind the house one of the trees, somewhat constrained in the small available space, was spreading its slightly drooping side branches over the roof, and its fruits hung round and dark, creating a pattern against the blue. Some had fallen onto the ground and had been rolled by the wind onto the garden gravel and the road. Once, just outside the gate, I found one and took it home.

"O blessed angels of Paradise, it's a nettle tree!"

The sight of the fruits has Maddalena weep even more than usual.

"My poor husband planted one in our house at Ferrovieri when our first child was born, may Heaven guard him among its angels. He said it reminded him of his land, he came from the lowlands, but from a nice place, full of trees. He had chosen Ferrovieri because it was green and the river widens spaces, he said. And he always used to say that the children could climb the nettle tree, because it has solid branches, not like the cheating fig tree that will crack even when it's big. And then it's a holy tree, the nettle tree is – they also call it the rosary tree, because you can make rosary beads from the fruits. If you find me sixty or so, I will make you one: I know how."

No-one could ever be seen in the garden or inside the house, even though the light was always on, signalling some sort of presence.

Once I was forced to stop in front of the gate. Through the closed windows I could hear a piano played with a sound I could not recognise. I could not tell who the composer or the musician might be. It was not the unmistakable touch of my teacher, which had a brilliancy and a slight unconscious tendency to draw long waves of sounds, something that could barely be perceived: although the notation and expression of the score were respected, the entire sonority of the piece would rise and fall as if imitating a cradling movement of which he evidently was not aware. By contrast, the sound I could hear as I stood in the street was assured, unhesitating, but disordered. It was clear that the duration of the notes was not as it should be: they were slightly too long, or a little too brief. One was tempted to interrupt the playing and clean it up. Yet this was not the insecurity of a beginner: it had a kind of logic – and then, the music did not come to any end. There were no movements, no pauses. It was as if flowing in fits and starts around a basic theme that was precise although never wholly formulated. There was something bewitching in that sound, as note after note it promised a resolution that never came.

I stood outside the gate for a long time, my scarf fluttering around me in the wind. But the music did not stop.

"It was my mother at the piano, yesterday afternoon."

Maestro De Lellis is as courteous as ever as he speaks, his back turned while he takes a score from the chair.

I am plunged deep into a shame that I had never known before in his presence.

I had been walking past his house and stopping just outside for weeks: impossible to think he had not noticed me.

"When I am not teaching, I spend all my time with her. She is not well. She was once a concert pianist." His tone is somewhat apologetic. "If you would like to, Signorina, you may come in tomorrow. You could give me your opinion on the piano: your excellent ear could be of help to us. There is something in that piano that disturbs my mother, but neither I nor the tuner are able to tell just what it may be."

"What about that music?"

"That is a story I will tell you some time."

"What about the swaying chandelier?"

"You shall see."

Seventeen

I went with Maddalena, who had been adamant.

"A young lass does not go alone to visit a man." In her anxiety, having to contradict me, she finds again words from her native dialect.

"But his mother's there."

"Yes – but will she be *all* there? Even as a young girl she was a wild little thing."

"Then you know her! What do you know about her?"

"Nothing – graveyards are overflowing with those of too much knowing."

The door was opened by Maestro De Lellis, who was not at all surprised to see Maddalena, but could not properly do the honours.

"Iis there someone at the door Aliiberto, iis someone there? Doo come in! Glaad to see you, very glaad!"

The words came from the first floor, quietly drizzling down a wide staircase of polished wood that curled around itself rather heavily, forming a half-spiral. It was a voice of music, gentle, made of quavering notes set apart by intervals of one tone. She was singing rather than speaking, but sounding wholly unlike what I usually heard from the pupils of singing classes at the *conservatoire*. Now I know that it was something similar to monastic cantillation. And the words had the extraordinary pattern of the music I had heard the day before, the duration of sounds splayed out across a phrase, following an inner melody entirely its own.

"We are coming, Mamma. Do play if you like, while you wait for us."

At that moment a music started, entirely different from the one I had heard the day before, but with the same outlandishly anarchic and yet mesmerising pattern.

"Doctors think it might be a singular, anomalous form of Pick's Disease," Maestro De Lellis says calmly. "I would define it as a sort of personal, musical version of the disease. She only has very long-term memory – memories of her childhood and adolescence – and, if I may put it that way, a *working*, short-term memory. Very short-term, in her case."

"Is the music hers?" I say.

"She will start from a theme of her own invention. At times it is possible to recognise some parts of the famous pieces she has played throughout her life. She will look at her hands and remember some of the notes she has just played, but not the correct sequence of their duration – and so she will make small variations on that theme, hooking onto the last notes she can remember, but with continual changes to the duration. We may perhaps define it as a sort of *terza rima* as applied to music – only written in free verse."

"She could read from scores," I say, still trying to understand.

"She no longer likes to do so. She will . . . wrap herself in her music. It's the disease. There are those who cannot stop talking: she plays. This peculiar form has been the subject of much study, as it were: several neurologists have asked for recordings of her music. And she does the same with words."

"Tears your heart out, this music does," Maddalena says as she dries her eyes.

"Not always: it depends on the initial theme. Sometimes I will suggest one to her – something lighter."

"Does she ever stop?" I ask, recalling the afternoons I have spent listening.

"She does when I ask her to, or when she has slowed down too much and cannot recall the last notes: often, then, she will be unable to start again of her own accord. Some other times she can."

He was in no hurry to go upstairs. The front room was very beautiful. The three large windows overlooking the front court-yard were matched by three more at the back of the house, which was dominated and somewhat darkened by the huge mass of the nettle tree. Most of the room was taken up by a monumental sofa with a white cover and two *bergère* armchairs upholstered in a shot fabric patterned with roses. But the most astonishing feature of the room were its walls, entirely covered in photographs alternating with portraits, all showing the same woman, now young, now more mature, in some cases already on the verge of old age. Always sitting at the piano, on stage, in the act of playing. No family photographs.

"Your mother," I say.

"Yes. So that she may remember herself as she once was," Maestro De Lellis says apologetically. "The sickness has . . . robbed her of the best memories in her life. Not even her successes were spared. She has nothing left."

The pictures had not been arranged in any order: some very large ones next to tiny ones, next to oil, charcoal or pencil portraits. Nearly all the photographs were in black and white: she evidently loved to dress in white, and shone as if gliding over the black background of the piano, the concert hall, the stage. She seemed to glow with an inner light, radiant with the beauty that comes from feeling oneself important, part of something that has value and brings happiness.

"She's an angel, just as everyone used to say." To dry her tears today, Maddalena has brought a snow-white little handkerchief of finest cotton muslin.

"Critics liked to call her 'the angel of the piano'. They would say that she had an angel's name: Gabriella De Lellis. And she did indeed always dress in white."

"De Lellis," I say, involuntarily repeating the Maestro's words.

"Yes. I know nothing of my father. When I was a child, she would tell me that I had two mothers: herself and music. Later, she promised that one day she would tell me everything. Then she fell ill – but I have the good fortune of not entertaining any curiosity."

"Curiosity is a sister to the devil," Maddalena says approvingly.

We climbed the stairs in silence, instinctively tiptoeing so as not to disturb that tranquil drizzle of notes echoing from one wall to the other, from one floor to the other, thanks to acoustics that I perceived as flawless.

She did not look up. She was sitting at the piano and looking at her pale fingers as they glided all along the keyboard like young girls at play on the beach. She was following them with the care of a childminder responsible for their movements, pleased with them and at the same time apprehensive lest one or the other should escape. Her full-length white dress was fluttering in a breeze, revealing a well-rounded, softer and more maternal body than shown in the photographs on the ground floor. There was nothing dry about her: for once, Maddalena had been wrong.

"The chiild from the hoouse on the riiver," she says softly in a singsong voice, without lifting her eyes from the keyboard.

Maestro De Lellis stops dead in the middle of the room.

"Then you remember her, you remember what I told you . . ."

"I reemember the sohrrow of women who aare mothers to beeloved children."

"Did you know my mother?" I say anxiously.

"Too many questions make for bad answers," Maddalena says, immediately cutting me short. "There's a breeze in here . . ."

Maddalena wants to change the subject fearing I might be indiscreet, but it is true that a swirl of air is coming from somewhere, and making us shiver even though we are still in our coats.

The light-filled room was almost wholly taken up by the grand piano, surrounded by three large *ficus benjamina* whose leaves were quivering softly, rustled by a slowly revolving wooden fan suspended from the ceiling and almost completely hidden by the plants. The glass chandelier also participated in that quiet movement, which I had noticed from the street on my afternoon walks.

"My mother needs the breath of the world around her," Maestro De Lellis says softly. "She once used to walk for hours: to Parco Querini in the city, or the park of the Villa Guiccioli, not far from here, above the Basilica of Monte Berico."

"She used to come to Ferrovieri, too, along the Retrone."

Maddalena is not sure she wants to speak. She stops and watches her playing, waiting for some sort of assent that does not come.

"It was raining, the first time I saw her. You could see her from far off. She was walking along the river bank and her white dress was flying about her, at first. She was looking in front of herself without noticing how the rain was making her skirt heavier and heavier. I had the impression she was talking to someone: an angel talking to her fellows."

"I did not know that. I would not have thought she would walk out that far. On the other hand, that is a typical symptom of her illness, this restless wandering," the Maestro says.

"But it's not far: you can take the path that goes down to San Giorgio, it's very quick."

"I don't know it, she never took me there . . ."

"Perhaps it was one of her secrets," Maddalena says in a conclusive tone.

While playing, Signora De Lellis was following my movements around the room. I was accustomed to feeling people's eyes on me, and could tell whether their gaze was moved by curiosity, disgust, compassion or – sometimes – benevolence. In this case, it was interest. This was not the wan stare of a weak-minded elderly lady: she knew me, knew who I was, or at least I reminded her of something definite, a remembrance whose fragments she did not have to struggle after as they drifted around, unmoored in her memory.

I could hear nothing wrong with the piano. It was an extraordinary Steinway, perfectly tuned – and I did not have to try and find any possible fault with it: when, as suggested by Maestro De

Lellis, I moved closer to examine its mechanism, his mother leant forward slightly, as if looking for inspiration, and whispered in my ear, without any lilting or singing vowels:

"Ring the bell tomorrow. I'll be waiting."

Eighteen

I was alone in Contrà Riale. I no longer had any news of Lucilla.

One morning, in the summer months between primary and secondary school, I had found Maddalena in the kitchen, slumped at the breakfast table and sobbing breathlessly.

"You're not going to see Lucilla for a while," she says, her nose plunged in the large, pink polka dot handkerchief she keeps for the occasions that require many tears.

I did not know what to think: I had seen Lucilla only the day before. My startled movements had the tea rocking in my cup as I replaced it on the table and sat down.

"What do you mean? We're all going to the Arena this evening. You're coming too . . ."

"She went away. Miss Albertina called at six o'clock this morning."

"Went away? At six o'clock in the morning?"

"She did. May the good Virgin of Monte Berico protect her. Her Mamma was arrested."

Maddalena sits up, props her elbows on the table and takes her head into her hands.

"Arrested."

"Miss Albertina said that her husband, Lucilla's father, the one who'd been making love to a lass who wasn't yet of age, came back last night, and she killed him."

"Killed him! But how?"

"Threw him from the balcony. He fell into the river."

"The river!"

"The other river," Maddalena says, hearing the words I have not spoken. "The Bacchiglione. It was in self-defence, Miss Albertina says. He was drunk. But even so they've arrested her, of course. It's always a woman's fault over here."

"Over here?"

"Yes, over here, in our saintly-Catholic-apostolic-gossip-holic town of priests and nuns. Did you know that in proportion we have more of them here than there are in Rome? One day the Holy Virgin will look down and turn us all to ashes, just like Sodom and Gomorrah. For all its shop windows and great houses gleaming like crocodile scales, this town has a soul black as the waters of the Retrone that swallowed up your Mamma, the poor young Signora, so young and so unhappy."

"What happened to Lucilla?"

"Miss Albertina sent her away to take her out of the storm. Much too much talk."

"Away where?"

"*Mah!*" Maddalena says by way of an answer.

"How long for?"

"Who knows?"

"What about school? Is she not coming to secondary school with me?"

"I'm afraid the waters will hardly be any calmer by September."

"What about me?"

Nineteen

"To the house of Maestro De Lellis? Why on earth? He does after all share his art with you during your lessons, twice a week . . ."

My father was displeased with that first visit to the Maestro's house. Over the last few months, he had been paying more attention to my life than usual. I could sense that he too was frightened of secondary school. He was trying to understand what missing Lucilla might mean to me, and perhaps to himself as well. Lucilla had been for him a guarantee that he would come to know everything, absolutely everything, that might happen to me. Whenever she stayed with us for supper, she would talk with the same ardent gusto that she showed for food. Displaying the wide-eyed innocence of a Tiepolo *putto*, she would mix in a totally unmediated way what may be said, what is best left unsaid and what must absolutely not be said, and no-one seemed to find anything inappropriate in her unconventional talk.

"Pick's Disease," Maddalena says, reading from a note she has made on a scrap of paper after returning from our visit. "Is it dangerous?"

"Not to others," my father says, addressing Maddalena's fears more than her words. "She will get lost if she goes out, won't be able to find her way, might even forget her own name. There are some who have been found miles and miles away from their homes."

"The old Signora has something inside her that's more frightening than what the young Signora had," Maddalena says. She looks at my father, who is waiting to hear the rest. "The young Signora, who is surely sitting next to the Virgin as we speak, she knew everything, saw everything, never missed even one single word, I know that for sure. She was just sad, that's all: sadness had wormed its way right through her soul without anyone realising, not even you, our poor Doctor. Like furniture that has only a few holes you can see from outside, but inside it's been eaten through by woodworm and will crumble into pieces if you so much as touch it. That's how it happened. Truth is, the soul of your young Signora just crumbled to pieces that night on the balcony, and she fell, she just fell. But old Signora De Lellis, her mind is withdrawn, like a snail in its shell. And no-one knows what might be inside."

"And my Signora – what was in her mind?"

"Everything. She knew everything, and her head was full of fear. You can't know everything and carry on living."

"In any case it is not necessary for you to go and see Signora De Lellis again," my father says conclusively.

Twenty

I went back the following day, as she had asked. The chandelier was trembling but there were no lights on. Someone opened the gate as soon as I rang the bell. I climbed the three steps to the front door. She was there, hardly any distance back from the threshold. I could see the whiteness of her dress from behind the opaque glass panes. Either she had been waiting, I thought, or she was far more agile than she showed herself to be. At the last moment, I hesitated, slightly afraid, and so she opened the door.

"Here is Rebecca – she who snares all men!" she says with a smile.

I do not understand her: the words she is articulating, very clearly, in a loud voice and with perfect rhythm, frighten me as if they had been conjured through some unknown sorcery. Neither am I clear about their meaning.

"Rebecca is a Hebrew name, it comes from the Bible: she was Isaac's wife, a young and very beautiful woman. It means 'a woman who is well-liked by men'. That's what your name says."

I am at a loss, and suddenly feel hurt at the thought that my name carries my mother's sorrow.

"Did your mother choose it?" she says, as if she were looking through a window into my feelings.

"I don't know." It is true that I know nothing of my own name. Aunt Erminia told me no stories about it. But I think, perhaps Signora De Lellis does know something.

"Hush! All in good time. All in good time. Things are not always as they seem."

As she spoke, she led the way up the staircase. She moved with ease despite her age, and not even the fact that she certainly was heavier than the pictures on the ground floor showed could stop her walking as if dancing, gliding just above the floor.

"I'm not as old as you think," she says with amusement, turning to look at me. "You see me as old because you are so young, and also because Maddalena, like everyone in town, calls me 'the old Signora'. And don't ask me how I know – the world is full of people who want to know everything, absolutely everything. Wives want to know about their husbands' cheating. Do they feel any better for it? Absolutely not. People who are engaged try to find out about any previous love stories. What vulgarity! As if we were not born anew each day, each moment. That's what sets us apart from animals, the ability to change constantly. If there is one true thing the Gospel says, it's that there is a new life behind every corner. It's never over, never – remember that."

She sits on the top step, spreading her dress out around her.

"I do get tired climbing the stairs, as a matter of fact. If only I could go out like I used to! But they won't let me, you see. Because of this Pick's Disease thing: they say I would get lost. Just imagine! I know this town like my own piano. But do take your coat off: it's hot in here, because I don't like heavy clothes. It's really hot today."

I helped her to get up. Her hands were as soft as her son's, and the contact left a scent of lavender and vanilla on my fingers.

She smiled at me again, complicitously, and started playing a Chopin prelude. At the end of that first one, after a brief pause, she played the second, then the third. I already knew how to recognise greatness: she was still an outstanding concert pianist, and would easily have been able to tour the world if she had wanted to. Or else to teach.

I wait for the next pause and say:

"It's always you playing in the afternoon. They're not records. Sometimes you play normally and sometimes you . . . you don't."

"Ah-ah! You understand. Between pieces, I try to play regularly, so those who hear me from the street will think it is a recording. But not when Aliberto is here."

"Why not?"

"You play now!"

She got up to let me sit at the piano. The scent of talcum powder.

"I like mixing perfumes," she says as she sinks into the armchair beside the piano.

"Can you read people's minds?"

"I too am sensitive to smells."

Twenty-one

And so when it happened there was no-one for me to turn to. Ironically, it was in the music room – a room that stood isolated on the first floor landing, its name written in faded China ink copperplate on a label stuck to the old wood that no-one ever cared to polish. It was not used very often, and that was why it had been chosen. The first thing one could notice on entering was a set of slender fold-up music stands. That day I counted them, there were twenty-five. They were ranged in a semicircle on the left-hand side of the room, precariously balanced on their brittle metal legs. Mutilated spiders, I thought. They could be folded and taken to a concert, but there was no music group in that school – perhaps there had never been one. Perhaps some eager teacher had ordered them just before being sent away. On the right, tucked away in a corner, was an old harmonium resting on a valuable little table that had somehow remained in the school. It was a mirror-topped art deco table, its curved legs tapering down with slightly canine grace. I knew its style, it was the same as the little dressing table in my mother's bedroom. Absurdly enough, there was a teacher's desk in that room, and a wooden chair complete with armrests. On the teacher's desk was a basket with six pairs of colourful maracas, of the kind used in nursery schools, with little enamelled pictures. One pair had two stubby Latin American dancers, dressed in red on a yellow background and wearing large brown sombreros. Their bellies coincided with the widest part of the maracas, which made them look obese. The other maracas were bright green with red, blue, purple and orange four-leaf clovers. Disused toys more than musical instruments.

All students to assemble in music room during break for update.

The notice on the blackboard is from the class prefect: I recognise his spiky scrawl.

I had hardly ever entered the music room during my three years at secondary school. One more week, and I would never have entered it again. If I had happened to fall ill during those last days of the school year, no-one would have been able to entice me into that place again. There is no master plan, life happens by chance, it is by chance that life may be good, decent, bad, unspeakable. One is saved because of a key that might not have been in the lock that day. One is ruined because Albina the beadle has left it there by mistake, or out of indolence, or sloppiness, or excess fat. The idea came that morning, because the key was seen in the lock. An idea without a starting history.

Twenty-two

"If I'd been in class with you that would never-ev-er-have-hap-pened."

Lucilla is pale, and life has made her incredibly slimmer than she once was. She appeared on my doorstep one day, quite unexpectedly, after everything had happened, and here she is now, more than ten years late for our outing to the Arena. She is sitting on the armrest of the little chair placed between the piano and the enamelled wood stove, a lovely girl dressed in an acid green skirt suit so full of character that it manages not to clash with the dark and light blue tones in the room. Her hands are abandoned on either side of the armchair, and she is listening to what I am telling her as the cool, almost autumnal wind blows the curtains in and out of the windows. She is listening and waiting, because I am speaking and playing. More playing than speaking.

She never failed to know anything even before people finished thinking of it. Curious, nosy, gossipy, healthy, beautiful, round Lucilla. Nothing would have gone wrong if she had been with me, I know.

Twenty-three

"Shut the door, monster."

The music room also had thirty ugly, green formica chairs, disused and dumped there from some other classroom. They could be counted quickly, in rows of five, in the middle of the room. In the glass cabinet propped against the right-hand wall, scattered haphazardly on three grimy shelves, were three metronomes, one clarinet, three oxidised transverse flutes, seven worthless white and brown plastic recorders. I could see their black finger stops, level with my eyes, on the second shelf from the top.

"Shut the door, you hairy monster."

On the bottom shelf of the cabinet, a wooden xylophone, its black paint chipped away at the striking points.

Not all of them have come: some did not dare. Or perhaps felt pity. I can count seventeen shadows: three are missing.

A beam of light comes through the high window over the door and dies on the dusty glass pane of the cabinet. On the left, just above the lock, the print of five fingers: one boy has tried to open the cabinet by putting his hand on the glass.

"I have beautiful hands," I am thinking. I try to look for my hands but cannot see them: they are behind my head, where they have told me to put them.

There are days born under the sign of a promise, but that means nothing at all. That morning the sun was shining, and before leaving for school I had opened the windows wide in the salon, so as to let in the midsummer heat that would dry the damp rising from the black river.

I have no theories about God, I cannot say whether or not he exists. Nor do I know whether he is good rather than almighty. Surely, if he is there at all, he is at times desperately absent-minded.

Twenty-four

"You smell like fritters," Signora De Lellis says as she opens the door on a February afternoon.

"Aunt Erminia brought some at lunchtime," I say.

"Uh! Madama Erminia!"

"Do you know her?"

"Everyone in town knows her."

"How do you know that?"

"Up to two years ago I used to go out, to walk. Every day, way up to the Piazzale of Monte Berico, as far as the park, or down towards the Retrone. But play me something now."

She would sit behind me after opening a score on the music stand.

"I don't need it," I say, as I do each time.

And as each time she replies: "Yes you do. What does my son teach you? And besides I like turning the pages, they smell good."

I would play on as her calm voice continued talking. She would suggest a *rallentando* or a different way to take a trill, she would ask me to repeat a *finale* or review the ways in which various concert pianists had approached a certain *presto*. I was astonished at how an adult could talk so much: Lucilla had accustomed me to inhabiting her swarms of words, but I had thought that a peculiarity of her own, the hallmark of a profligate child. At home one would only speak in order to inform, communicate or decide. At mealtimes, even in winter, it was easy to hear moorhens glide on the waters of the Retrone as they sifted through surface weeds. My mother's silences had saturated the whole house, the river into which she had slipped, and ultimately all our lives. Speaking was an effort, it called for overcoming resistance not only from the air, but from our souls.

"Do not think of sorrows now, river child. This is a waltz: a dance meant for festivals to propitiate courtship and marriage. Your heart must follow the music, not the other way round."

"So you really can read people's thoughts."

"No – but I could smell river weeds."

Twenty-five

The lady in white became part of my life at once. School, meals and homework now were for me only interludes between visits. I would go three times each week, on the afternoons that Maestro De Lellis spent teaching at the *conservatoire*, to play and to listen to her. At a stroke she had replaced Lucilla, Aunt Erminia and even my mother. The little black dot in the corner of my eye turned into the white cloud of her light garments made for an everlasting summer.

My father did not know, and neither did Aunt Erminia, who often would not come back until late in the evening. Maddalena did know, but she kept the secret, albeit with much anxiety.

"What is it you do all afternoon with the old Signora? She's not all there, and can't play very well by now, the poor thing. Does she give you tea at least? What about Maestro De Lellis? Is he there too?"

"She's not that old, and she plays very well sometimes. I talk to her about school, about music – and I play too, you know. I go on the days when the Maestro is at the *conservatoire*. And anyway, what are you scared of, Maddalena?"

"You never know what people might have in mind," she says sharply.

In actual fact, it was Signora De Lellis who did all the talking. She told me the story of each and every one of the pictures on the wall. The one from the Concorso Busoni, the competition she had won at eighteen, which had taken her "around the world on the wings of a score": Milan, Vienna, Berlin, Paris. And then New York. Next to it were pictures from all the concerts in that year, she standing radiant to the left of the piano, her hands open in front of her in a gesture of greeting but also of self-protection. The dress was always the same: white tulle, with a narrow waist and the skirt fanning out around her tiny, fairy-like feet.

"My parents tried to make me change it, because it would always look like the same concert in the press. But I said it brought me good luck and absolutely refused," Signora De Lellis says as she strokes the dress in the photographs.

In New York, the dress was different: a white satin fabric sliding loosely over her body and highlighting the soft curve of her hips. Her hands too were in a different position, joined in front of her chest as if in prayer.

"I had to change my dress that time," she says with some amusement. "I was pregnant already, and could no longer fasten the other one. Luckily my parents only realised when it was too late – or God knows what they would have forced me to do! I was under age at the time: it was a scandal. Uh! What a scandal! A ruined career, they all said. A wasted promise. It was the talk of the town, and the province, and eventually the national press. And they all wanted to know about the child's father – to hold him to his duties, they said. His duties! What petty, office-clerk language to speak of love and life. What they really wanted was to find him and throw him into jail. Back then, it was a crime to seduce – that was the word – an under-age girl. Unless the man was rich, of course, in which case, provided he married the girl, honour was saved, or just about. Honour. My mother was so ashamed that she never set foot outside the house again, and she locked me up too."

"Like my mother," I say, interrupting.

"Not yet, darling, not yet. All in good time. It's a matter of understanding whether the truth will do good or just hurt. Truth is not as necessary as priests would have us believe, you know."

But she liked to speak. So I learnt that her mother had not died "of a broken heart", as everyone had said, but of alcoholism. The shame she felt when her daughter became pregnant might have worsened things, but she had been drinking for a long time, at least since "marrying up" and becoming the lady of the ancient villa that dominated the city from its high position, just as its owners had. They had been notaries, in the profession for generations, calculating keepers of the hatreds that set whole families and estates crumbling. And her father had died for the same reason: he had not killed himself for love, but crashed drunkenly into the glass cabinet in the salon. It was she who had found him, already dead at the bottom of the stairs: he had fallen and bled to death while looking for help. One could certainly not speak of such an improper thing. The suicide for love was a story she had invented: she the young, romantic pianist who had just become a mother and was now suddenly orphaned, rich and free. Free to go out, to play music and to create a legend that might have her pilloried in our small town, but gave tragic stature to her concerts abroad. "The sad angel" of the keyboard. In its craving for sorrowful narratives, the town soon reversed the sequence of events, and the pianist with the melancholy touch, orphaned and *then* seduced

121

and jilted, finally won its narrow provincial heart, erasing any memory of past shame.

"I returned to the New York stage two years later, with a light, brilliant Mozart programme – but even then the papers said that my interpretation revealed to the sensitive listener the sorrow at the source of my talent," she says with amusement one day, showing me a photograph taken from the corner of the stage, in which the corolla of an almost nuptial white dress opens out around her as she bows in front of an enraptured audience.

I know I will never in my life play on a stage, and for once, treacherously, the thought stabs its way into my feelings.

"Success is like a river in spate," the old Signora says. "It will burst into your life out of the blue, and when it's gone, you'll have to rebuild everything."

Twenty-six

I did not have the courage to ask any questions, but in her ceaseless flow of words she would let fall some hint or sign that would lead me back in time, back to when my mother was alive, back to things I had failed to notice even though I wore out my days in the effort to listen, to miss nothing about her life.

One day, during the following autumn, it became clear that she had known my mother.

She had asked me to play Mendelssohn's "Venetian Barcarolle". I was surprised: it was a much easier piece than any I would usually bring to her. I know now that I was not playing it properly, having learnt it by ear from Aunt Erminia's exaggeratedly slow and sentimental version.

Signora De Lellis was sitting behind me.

"Is this the way you used to play it for your mother?" she says.

"Not for . . . for her. Not only for her. I played it because Aunt Erminia liked it. I don't know if my mother, if she . . . was listening to it, if she liked it at all. I . . . we had no way of knowing. She would not ask . . . she never did."

"Neever." She reverts to her cantillation at times, when she has something important to say.

"Never. She never spoke about us, about me or anything to do with me." I am choosing the most neutral words, so as not to make her suspicious, so as to keep that open chink in her narration. I want her to speak, and fear anything I say might wake her from the gentle rocking motion of her memories.

"She adored this 'Barcarolle'," she says.

"Adored it?"

"When they can't speak, women write, remember. How long has it been?"

"A year," I say, without her needing to be any clearer.

"One year, seven months and seventeen days."

"Is that so?"

"It is."

She said nothing more. She stood up from her armchair and walked once around the room, looking for something. Then she opened the first drawer in a polished briarwood wardrobe, and from a flat gilt box took a huge white fan that she started slowly waving in front of the mirror hanging on the opposite wall. The fan moved noiselessly, like angels' wings breezing past.

"It's made of ostrich feathers," she says without looking at me, the fluttering of her hair and her dress enhancing the image of a cloud. It was easy to follow her luminous shadow as it moved around me. Speak, I wanted to say. Tell me. Tell me what you know. If I can play this piece to perfection she might tell me. I know how to keep secrets, I am kneaded from the very stuff of secrets, I myself am a monstrous family secret, a secret of nature, a universal secret. I mustn't get that note wrong, I mustn't I mustn't. If I play well she'll tell me, if I don't look at her she'll tell me, if I don't ask she'll tell me, if I make no mistakes she'll tell me. My fingers are flying, they know these notes, I have played them countless times. Perhaps I had understood my mother liked them, perhaps that was the reason. Or was it for Aunt Erminia? Steady, you gruesome hairy monster. That's what Beatrice called me in class this morning. I can hear everything, I can see. They think being ugly also means being deaf and blind. She smelled like blood as she talked to Federica, like the fillet steak Maddalena beats with her tenderiser before cooking it – there, I've messed up now. Too slow this finale, too too slow. You stupid hairy monster, the old Signora has stopped speaking.

"Have you gone into your mother's room since?" she says in the end.

"No, I haven't."

"Then it's time you did. Don't you think so?"

Twenty-seven

Maddalena did go into my mother's room after her death. That day, the wind was raging at the curtains of the French window leading to the little balcony from which she had fallen.

From the doorway I had seen Maddalena tidying away the traces of the police who had left everything thrown open, rummaged through, mixed up, scattered around. Stockings with books, ribbons with light bulbs, dresses with notebooks with perfumes. Most of those things I had never seen before. I knew none of her perfumes.

Maddalena began from the wall to the left of the door. She was placing books back onto the empty shelves, picking them up from the floor according to size: the tallest ones first, and gradually down to the smallest. She would dust them one by one, now and again stopping to dry her tears as they fell like raindrops onto the covers. If she spotted a mistake in the downward order she was building, she would move one book or another. Then she turned to the wardrobe. The clothes were all heaped on two small white armchairs. So it was that I saw the sky-blue wedding dress. The tight corset was held up by two slender satin ribbons. The skirt, hardly widening as it fell in the shape of a bellflower, was enriched by some deep pleats opening onto a white fabric embroidered with cornflowers, their fringed petals interweaving in a game of rainbow threads. Maddalena also retrieved from the floor a weightless white stole edged with tiny embroidered cornflowers.

The dress had been a present from the Carmelite nuns of Monte Berico.

"It's worth a fortune," Aunt Erminia says one day, in the mood for talking about the wedding. She is speaking in a loud voice, so that my mother can hear from her little drawing-room. "Fully hand-stitched – every single thread. And for free. Your mother used to win people over just like that. She was like the Pied Piper. She would pass by, all dressed in white, and even flowers would bow on their stems."

Suddenly Maddalena had turned towards me as I stood in the doorway, my feet as if cemented to the floor, and looked at me in despair. Then she had started scooping up great armfuls of things at random. Clothes, shoes, papers, notebooks, all stuffed at raging speed into drawers, crammed into the dresser, shoved under the bed. She would throw everything in, level the top with her hands, and close. The desk lamp ended up in the trunk, the pictures under the bedspread, the hair brushes, bedside clock and lingerie into the dresser drawers. Until everything was shut away, or put under.

"Why?" I ask.

"The dead are like shoes," Maddalena says. "Each to his own, or they'll hurt too much."

Before leaving the room she closed the balcony shutters and the window, drew the curtains and smoothed them with her hands so they would fall back down in regular folds.

Twenty-eight

During my first two years at secondary school, I had sometimes tried to ask Maddalena what had become of Lucilla. The solitude of my endless mornings at the classroom desk in Contrà Riale wore down my ability to bear with my nostalgia for those huge tides of words with which, throughout primary school, Lucilla had pulled me into her world, and thanks to that, into the world at large.

I often caught myself thinking she might have been trying to look for me. I no longer knew anything of her: not where she might be, not why she was not writing or calling me. I imagined situations that would make it impossible for her to make contact: far away perhaps, perhaps on the other side of the world? Or in prison, even? Under no circumstance, though, did my doubts ever turn into resentment: I knew that her silence must have a reason, and that only my ignorance of things was keeping it from me.

One day, by chance, I learnt from Maddalena that Miss Albertina had found a teaching post outside town. After the end of primary school I had never seen her again, and yet the certainty that she too, like Lucilla and her mother, was now someone I could no longer meet quite unexpectedly, perhaps in Corso Palladio or Piazza Matteotti, gave me a feeling of unbearable loneliness.

"Will Lucilla at least come back?" I say to Maddalena one evening. All through the day I had been trying to find the courage to ask, going into the kitchen on the pretext of a second cup of tea, a glass of water, an offer of help in baking the biscuits. I would have wanted to ask at suppertime, so as to stop Maddalena rushing off with the excuse of some errand, but Aunt Erminia had appeared that evening with stories, more and more stories to tell.

And so the question had come late, sharp with urgency and also with fear of the possible answer, hardly an instant after Maddalena had turned the lights out at bedtime. Sheltered by darkness.

"People do what they can. And sometimes a thousand years are like one day."

"Sometimes when?" I say, undaunted.

"When people have to fight."

Maddalena too is speaking sharply: she does not know how to be elusive, and if ever she has to be, finds it very hard. Perhaps she has no answer, or none that may reassure me.

The present evil was the indifference that surrounded my life. Aside from Maddalena, who could sense the unfairness of that isolation but had no way of breaking it, neither my father nor Aunt Erminia seemed to be aware of it. And so at times, with shocking suddenness, that imperviousness to feelings into which people accustomed to sorrow constrain themselves gave way to a bitter nostalgia for the merry sound of Lucilla's steps ringing out next to mine on the paving stones of Corso Palladio. And that longing would cut my breath short.

Then my enquiries grew even more awkward, questions asked knowing full well it was no use:

"Why won't Lucilla call me? She knows where to find me." I

have stopped Maddalena halfway up the stairs, her arms full of freshly laundered linen.

"It is written: 'then go out of that city and shake the dust off your feet'," Maddalena says after a long silence. "Sometimes you have to leave like that."

"But I am not dust," I say, protesting without realising.

"We all are in the end," Maddalena says conclusively, turning around like she does when tears are too much even for her.

Twenty-nine

"I'd like the keys to her room," I say to Maddalena one day.

"It's open," she says from the kitchen, in a natural tone, as if she had been waiting every day for this moment to come.

I close the door behind me. No known smells to give me any sense of direction. My mother had no smell, or perhaps I had never been close enough to smell hers. In any case the room has been aired regularly. I open the curtains, the window, the balcony door. The world rushes at me. Smell of warm autumn rain. Faraway grapes, pomace, road dust, river weeds, feathers: they too are warm. I look down and see a moorhen: a doomed late brood, perhaps with no eggs laid. Smell of sweet pastry, lemon icing. My heart misses a beat – this is a memory: Lucilla's mother, the last cake she baked for me, before she left. The smell of books, old books, the Library, I walk past it every morning. The smell of Giardino Salvi, fine gravel and white swan feathers, of ring road, of motorway, of faraway snow on the mountains. I do not know my mother's smell.

I sit at her little dressing table, like she used to do. Women write, Signora De Lellis said. There is a mirror in front of me and I can see the door behind me. I realise how she would catch a glimpse of me whenever I glided quickly past her, ten times, a thousand times a day.

It is raining hard on the narrow stone balcony and on the river. The sound of a moorhen shaking water off her feathers.

Right-hand drawer. Black stocking, white stocking, white headscarf, light blue fountain pen, bone comb, hairpin, hairpin, hairpin, prayer book – prayer? Light blue stocking – light blue? Notebook. Blank. End of drawer.

Left-hand drawer. One blue skirt, fine pleated. Bunched up: Maddalena's fury. One flat black shoe. Smell of leather, also faint. Other flat black shoe. One blue notebook, an iris elegantly embossed on its hard cover. Writing.

First page: *Tiny pieces of sky are falling on me and cutting me all over.*

Thirty

I know all about sorrow.
It has the shape of the blood
that laid waste
my mother and father,
and the ancestors of dust and earth
and now me,
and still keeps me alive,
the smell of iron
that turns my nights to disgust,
the exact rhythm of steps
my steps
on marble
on wood
(on the street
when there was one),
the sound of your soft call
like a moorhen's cry.
Little girl from the house on the river
my silence is my shield.
Your shield.

six months five days three hours

Are these poems? I am reading my mother's diary with diffi-
culty. She writes in a pale blue China ink faded by time into all

shades of grey, almost invisible in places. Her handwriting is an astonishingly spiky microscript, made of tiny vertical strokes with few horizontal ones: a light step wandering across the page. There are no corrections. My mother thought carefully before she wrote.

> *Mostra whets her teeth on devoted flesh.*
> *Mostra walks at night to Monte Berico.*
> *Mostra a filthy stepmother*
> *plants sick cloven words around*
> *and stages for you*
> *lives that are not yours.*
> *The liar is blind with mercy.*
> *Any words might escape me*
> *would tear the bark off your soul.*
> *My silence is your salvation.*
>
> *three years eleven months two days*

Is Mostra Aunt Erminia? But why? Who is the liar? There are no dates. And why is my mother writing in such a difficult, cryptic way? Is she frightened?

> *From the river at night he caught sight of me*
> *and the crude silence he inflicts on me*
> *bled him of tiny*
> *rose-coloured tears*
> *Who seeded your*
> *promise? he asked*

his voice like a song
A god, was the reply
my silence gave at the end of the journey
There are no other gods before my plunging,
the mocking voice says
To be stone on the riverbed
is grace

six months six days six hours

Who speaks to my mother from the river at night? What are the references to time? I rush through the pages, trying to understand.

My little girl has returned to the house on the river. He tells stories into my silence and cannot see that it is nothing but waiting, and it won't come if I speak, even only one word, and neither will it come in silence, it won't come yet cannot but be awaited, because a promise was given to us and we believed in it, or perhaps we believed that someone had offered it especially to us and one must put oneself and one's life on hold and wait though nothing nothing seems to come and yet one would do anything to hasten its coming, anything, and one is frightened lest one might not hear its steps if the silence is less than perfect and the sacrifice less than total. For how can one accept that life will ravel shut just when it is most generously unfolding its promise?

five months two days

My age marks her days! I am her time-keeper. My mother did not write only poems. The mysterious writing speaks of my being here. And why are the dates not in order? I read at random into the diary looking for words that might cross with a memory, afraid I will not be able to recognise anything.

> She patters by, light on her
> soft little squirrel's feet
> and can't feel my silence stroking her.
>
> > four years two months twenty-nine days

My mother did see me, she wrote poems for me. I cannot stop reading and rereading these three verses that stroke my hair like her hearing me as I walked past her door, she with her back turned, facing this diary placed on the table.

> Mostra saw her hands yesterday. They are her hands, and his. The right number of fingers, not one too many. Hideous Mostra with her own perfect hands clawing at hers.
>
> > three years two months thirty days

"He" is my father. Women write, Signora De Lellis had said. How much did my mother write? Why did she hate Aunt Erminia? What happened, what could I not see?

> A mortal happiness
> shrugs our memories off
> one by one
> savage balance sheet
>
> > nine months

Is she delirious? And suddenly I understand the order. She first wrote in the right-hand pages of her little notebook, then when she got to the end started again on the left, and so anyone reading the diary through will lose track of time. I look for a day I may somehow be able to recall.

Little girl from the house on the river,
how many eyes touching you today
how many words will they say about you.
You too can see how silence is good and hurts less.
No-one comes to save us.
I cannot speak,
or see, or live, or feel,
I would lose my memory of you my little dream girl.
If I can keep you safe
when the night ends I'll give life, new, untouched life to you again.

six years five months twenty days

My time at school brings a shift in the writing, that turns subtler, more and more reticent: a dissolution of thought consuming itself in vowels reduced to tiny dots, word endings almost invariably left to the imagination.

Child Lucilla
you scatter words around
play ball with your own sorrow
Lucilla who sings and saves.

six years seven months one day

137

From this date onwards she has written in poetic form about Lucilla, Maddalena whom she calls Woman of Tears, the music I played, Aunt Erminia and a certain Lady of the Night.

Lady of the Night
your word touches me
in the flesh
but people fade away into things
little by little I'm turning to stone.
Lady of the Night
stubbornly speaking to me between rivers,
there is no bargaining
for wasted souls
only the god of water
black water
awaits them
stone moths on the riverbed.

seven years seven months two days

What woman spoke to my mother between the two rivers?

And Mostra laughs
her teeth sharpened on flesh she cannot have
she laughs and spreads scented slime around
masking the smell of sulphur
she laughs and the liar cannot stop
swinging the axe of his mercy.
He is spellbinding: wary, tentative spells drizzling down in pity to mourn
some little sorrow. But what am I saying, what — here is the servant of my

grieving, his grieving, the grieving of the flesh that the child alone is aton-
ing for on behalf of us all. So be it unto the ages.

seven years seven months eleven days

Many poems lose themselves after the first few verses, turning into alliterative games from which a thought suddenly emerges. A leap on the edge of lucidity. Then she plunges back down, each time just a little lower than before. Further on, she reverts to prose, but becomes incoherent.

The dressing gown belt showing from the wardrobe, trapped. The pocked stonework of the little balcony. A white kitten with her left back leg missing. The eye of a man on a little girl.

Hailstones piercing holes into the new green leaves of the elm trees. Yellow corolla pierced with holes by the sun. Flowers, painted on the pillars of a church, from afar they look like teeth, they are laughing the tongue blood red.

Is it possible to leave one's life and stay alive?

eight years seven months

She has kept to the sequence of dates, though. It's as if all her lucidity were concentrated there.

The Lady of the Night has left. She too into the silence. He calls from the black river with a rustle of tiny mice grooming themselves on a raft of algae. What else is there to say. The sorrow of not seeing her again. Never again my little girl of the house on the river. Unseemly weeping of time regret-ting its own existence.

Tiny pieces of sky are falling on me and cutting me all over.

nine years

I am reading the last page over and over again. How is it possible that nothing of these feelings for me could pass through into my life? Why did I not understand? Why did no-one understand?

Thirty-one

"Was mother mad?" I ask my father. I had been waiting for him in the hall, sitting in one of the little armchairs. First I had closed the doors to the other rooms, and opened the windows. The damp of the autumnal season mixed with the smell of river weeds was creeping up the stairs. Aunt Erminia was out. Maddalena was busy cooking.

"I don't think so – no." He is more resigned than surprised. He has hunched his handsome shoulders and put his doctor's briefcase on the first step of the stairs.

"Sit down," I say, pointing him to the other little armchair. He does. I have my mother's blue notebook in my hand.

"I gave it to her," my father says when he sees it.

"It's a diary," I say. He shows no surprise. "Did you know she kept a diary?"

"Yes, I did."

"It was in her dresser drawer. Unlocked."

"I never looked."

"Why not?"

"Out of respect, I think."

Neither of us spoke for many minutes. Outside, a sheldrake could be heard preening and washing his feathers in the river. The flutter of wings brought to mind the corolla of water spreading all around. The bells of Monte Berico were tolling six o'clock. The wind also carried the sugary scent of elm leaves in autumn.

"Do you want to read it?" I ask.

"No."

"It's hard to understand. Do you know what she called Aunt Erminia?"

"No."

"*Mostra*. Feminine of 'monster'. She hated her. Why?"

"I don't know."

I looked at him, trying to meet his eyes. But he was staring down at a spot on the floor, just beyond his soft moccasins that carried no imprint from his slim feet. Even after a day's work, he was elegant: his white shirt was not crumpled, his heavy blue linen trousers looked as if he had just stepped into them, his black hair seemed to have been combed one minute earlier in the bathroom at home. He sat in the little armchair with all the naturalness of tall and handsome men who seem to pass through any space hardly touching things, almost expecting everything to fit around them as a matter of course, as if the world had only been waiting for their passage to feel itself complete.

I thought of the way girls at school would talk about men, and I was struck by the idea that he must certainly be surrounded by women who were in love with him. Lucilla had said something about that when my mother died. But not one of them had ever called him at home, as far as I knew. Perhaps he had no other women after all, I thought. I was clutching the notebook with both hands and felt its cover slipping under my damp fingertips. I must have voiced my thoughts without realising:

"I have no other women," my father says.

"Why not?" I hear my own voice asking.

"Because I ruin everything I touch – that's why."

A pang of grief stabs through me.

"Is it me? Is it because of me?"

"No. It was because of me that your mother was . . . that way."

I waited for a few more words that did not come. When Maddalena came to look for me at suppertime, she found us both sitting still in the dark.

Thirty-two

Later that evening, I also questioned Maddalena. She was waiting for me in the kitchen, one elbow propped up on the table. Dishes and glasses were heaped on the dishwasher rack while the vanilla ice cream was melting in the tub left near the stove. She looked at me the whole time and answered me almost without crying – only, she was wringing her handkerchief in her hands.

Yes, she did know that the young Signora kept a diary, or that she wrote, at any rate, and she had also seen where she usually put her diary. Yes, she had told my father the doctor, and no, she did not know if he had read it or not. She could hear and see, but would not pry.

What did she think of my mother? That the young Signora needed help, a lot of help, and they gave her none, God forgive them. And no, absolutely not, in the Holy Virgin's name – she did not at all think it was my fault, that it was because of the way I looked that Mamma was like that. Some other terrible thing must have happened to her. In the beginning she had thought of something unspeakable between Madama Erminia and, God forgive her, my father. Why? Because Madama Erminia was too forward with him: because of the way she would brush against him as she passed behind him in the kitchen or on the stairs, because it was she who chose his perfumes, because of the way they would play the piano in the evening, tight next to each other, weaving their hands together, their shoulders touching. But in actual fact? In actual fact no, it was not so, she was sure of that just as you can be sure that Our Lord died on the cross for us all. There was a special bond between Madama Erminia and my father, a blood bond. They had been so at one before they were born that – how to put it – they were destined to chase after each other all their life, and when they were in the same room it was as if they were in the same womb, and their bodies were part of each other and you shouldn't be surprised about it or think any evil of it: it was nature, and she had understood that as she watched them both. And if in the beginning Madama Erminia had made her angry, now she only felt pity for her, because she was doomed to not ever find peace with any man, and to desire the only man she could never have, the poor, unfortunate woman. But why then was my mother like that? She did not know.

Once she had overheard her saying something to my father: yes, directly to my father, one night after he had spoken to her – enough to tear your heart out, may the Holy Virgin help us.

I was still a sorry little squirt rocking back and forth to find my balance. She was sitting in her usual armchair. One moment earlier I had slipped from Madama Erminia's control and fallen forwards, knocking my forehead against the marble floor, right at my mother's feet. She had not tried to help me up, had not made the slightest effort to stir, not moved a single muscle. Neither as I fell nor afterwards. And he, my father, had arrived at the right moment to see everything, may the Lord Jesus help us. And he had picked me up from the floor, and soothed me, and found ice for my bruised forehead, and I had finally calmed myself, bundled up in his arms like a sheldrake fledgling, only my little head peeking out from under the jacket he was still wearing – just like the sheldrakes on the river, only my little head to which my father was holding the ice.

And then? Maddalena paused in silence as she saw the scene again through my eyes. And then I had fallen asleep, and he had placed me in Maddalena's lap and taken my mother's hands, cupped them between his as one would cup water before drinking it, kissed them with tenderness and desire and then clasped them around her face, forcing her to look at him. But Mamma had closed her eyes. And then he had spoken to her all the same: "Life is not a precious object that we must guard through the years. Often, when it comes into our hands, it is chipped and cracked already, and we are not always given the pieces to fix it. Sometimes we have to keep it like that, broken as it might be. Sometimes we can remake the missing pieces together. But life is in front of us, behind us, above and inside us. It's there, even if you shy away and close your eyes and clench your fists. You are not alone: start over with us. We are there for you."

And then? And then, with her eyes closed and the voice of a robot, she had spoken to him: "What I have seen is not God. And now let me go."

No, Maddalena did not know what she might have meant, but it was clear that her rage was directed at my father, and to be perfectly honest she thought my mother really had not seen me fall, that she had just been deep in thought or dream, may the Holy Virgin help us. Surely we should have done something to help her – but nothing was done. Madama Erminia burned with her own fire, and she hated my mother, the young Signora, for stealing her brother and his love. Or perhaps for being more beautiful than her, of a different beauty that had more gentleness, more light – a bit like an angel, there, that's the word. And everyone loved her by "spontaneous motion", as Madama Erminia would say. And my father was scared of saying or doing anything. Maddalena could see him as he watched her from a distance, and it was clear that he would have wanted to do something. But what? Shake her, pull her out onto the little balcony in the wind and the rain, grab her by the shoulders and shake her until things fell back into place. But nothing, may the Holy Virgin help us. There he was, blocked like a broken clockwork cuckoo with its beak just out of the hatch and the voice forever caught in his wooden throat. Why? No reason why. People are born like that. Handsome or ugly, plucky or shy. That's nature for you.

Thirty-three

"Are you the Lady of the Night?"

The next day I had arrived at the nettle-tree house very early. Again Signora De Lellis was at the door, standing still in front of me, her usual quiet smile widening her round face that age had hardly creased.

"Yes. Your mother called me that ever since our first meeting."

"A night meeting?"

"Yes."

"Where?"

"Between the two rivers."

"I want to know," I say as I close the door behind me.

That day she did not walk upstairs as usual, but led the way into the kitchen, which opened onto the back of the house. It was a very light room despite overlooking the darkest part of the garden, where the rising ground climbed steeply forming a slope of shrubs and rocks, and where the nettle tree spread its thick branches casting shadow on the flowerbeds. On the garden side was a conservatory in which one could easily feel as if sitting outside, almost embraced by the branches of the huge tree. The wooden furniture, painted white, helped create an environment that seemed to radiate light.

That day, Signora De Lellis made tea for me.

"You always have tea at your house, don't you? So Aliberto tells me. And so also she told me – so she did."

"Then she did talk?" I ask.

"Yes, she did," Signora De Lellis says with a sigh.

She was sitting in front of me in a position I did not recognise. When she was telling me about the photographs or turning the pages of the scores I did not read from, her moving hands conveyed all the vitality of a restless existence that was not yet played out. But that afternoon she held her hands in her lap, the palms resting on the pleats of her dress, her fingers spread apart. Drawing deep into herself, she was trying to recall memories that would not wound me, to fill the gaps, make up for my missing memories, and she was doing so with concentration, aware that I would make those memories mine with the images, the colours, the nuances transmitted by her words. She knew that from that day on my mother would speak in her words and have the feelings that she ascribed to her. At that moment, she was birthing my mother for me. I had nothing at all to offset her descriptions, apart from some sentence spoken at mealtimes, a casual word now and again, the barbed hints from Aunt Erminia, the noise of a fall and a cry I had not heard.

"We met on a gloomy, moonless night. I often went out late at night, or very early in the morning. I was well, back then. I'm well now, you will say. But back then it was official. I was allowed out. You had been born a few months. She was fleeing fleeing fleeing, but really did not know what she was fleeing. She saw me sitting on the bench at the bottom of the street between the two rivers. I could clearly smell the strong scent of a brooding moorhen: the smell of warm feathers. She passes me and asks me if I have been sent by him. 'Him?' I ask. And she says: 'Yes, him.' We musicians, you know, are accustomed to meeting all sorts of original people. This young Signora in black, roaming the night alone, did not surprise me. After all that was what I did too. 'Yes and no,' I said to her. She touched me lightly, checking I was actually there: she was already unsure of herself at that time. But then, who knows! 'How do you mean, yes and no' she says. 'No, since to my knowledge at least, no-one sent me,' I reply. 'Yes, since I might be here because someone wants me to be. Some believe in that.' 'God?' she says, sorrow and irony in her voice. 'If he existed he should be fairly dismissed on the grounds of terminal incapability and absenteeism, after which he should be executed for cruelty and burnt at the stake for heresy against the truths he himself has proclaimed.' 'That's been done already,' I say. 'He's already been flogged and crucified and killed and buried.' 'But he lays claim to existence,' she replies, 'and savagely gorges on the desires that cut into our heart.'

"Then she sat on the bench, at the far end. And she started her story. No, she did not speak of you, child. She spoke of her family. Her parents were peasants, ashamed of the poverty sticking to everything like the greasy odour from the stables: to their clothes worn down until one could see through them, to their patched-up shoes, to their hair singed by the home-made hair styling. If they had to come to town to go to the doctor's, they would get up at daybreak to have a bath. At the last minute, just before leaving, they would iron the shirts they had brought in fresh from the morning sun. They would hurry on to the hairdresser's or the barber's. Then, in the hospital bathroom, before going in to see the doctor, they would scrub away at their nails again, one more time, fingers and toes, right there where the smell is like flypaper glue that won't come off even with thick bleach. And then every single time, at the end of the visit, as they fumbled for their wallet or took out their handkerchief, that smell would suddenly escape from the bottom of a handbag, thick and cloying, the unmistakable odour of cow dung, of straw festering under the hooves, of milk caked sour on the udders they had squeezed the day before. Like a wicked genie cooped up for too long, that smell rose above the scent of the freshly washed shirt, landed on top of the hairspray, mixed itself in with the surgery disinfectant and spread out into a cloud as big as the room, ready to fray into a lingering wake that followed them as they left."

Signora De Lellis paused and for the first time since I had met her I saw fatigue on her face. She took my hand and looked at it a long while, stroking my fingers.

"See, it's all about these – the fingers. It wasn't the stables: the true shame was in the taint. It was the taint they had to scrub off. It had always been there. It ran in both families, your grandmother's and your grandfather's. Sometimes children would be born with many fingers. They were normal, pretty as babies, and mentally healthy too. But they were locked away, out of ignorance, out of fear of prejudice and shame. And so they became ill. They grew stunted, rickety from knowing no sunlight, unable to speak from living in the stables with the animals. Sooner or later they would be killed by some disease, or by a horse kicking them as they slept between the hooves. Your grandfather did not tell your grandmother because he was afraid he might lose her, and your grandmother did the same. They had two boys, both with many fingers, so many you could not tell. Both died when they were very little, and someone must have known how, because after the death of the second one the mayor came, and the priest with him, and they said he'd better be the last one or next time the police would come instead. Then your grandparents finally made up their minds to go and see a doctor, and had no choice but to tell him that the many fingers ran in both families. He said it was hopeless, they should stop trying. But it was not easy to follow that sort of advice back then. Your mother was born after nine months of tears and novenas to the Virgin of Monte Berico, and it was a miracle. She had the right number of fingers, and was so beautiful that she always had pride of place in the living Nativity of their village: first the Christ Child, then a little angel in prayer, and later, when she was slightly older, the angel of ethereal light announcing salvation to the shepherds. And it was during a Christmas play that your father saw her: she was the Madonna, all dressed in white, her sky-blue veil studded with golden stars. He asked for her hand after the midnight mass. He was handsome, rich, he came from the city. But your grandparents were beside themselves with the fear that she might be cursed with the same fate as they had been, and the next day, as soon as they knew, they left just as they were – no fresh shirts, no hairdresser's. They walked into your father's town study and made him swear that his family had never had anyone born with more than ten fingers, or anyone a little 'behind', or anyone lame or deaf or cross-eyed, and that only good blood had been flowing in its veins for gen- erations and generations. And he gave his word. Then, kneeling in front of the two peasants, old and bent and laden down with guilt and fears as they were, he asked permission to marry your mother. Because love is like that, it has no memory and no future, it does not know that the days can awaken past histories."

Thirty-four

"What about me?" I ask the following day, at the end of a Schumann *Lied* that I have played with my whole soul hanging from Signora De Lellis's silent lips. She was moving around the room, rearranging a portrait on the wall or a score on a shelf, without pausing.

When her narration had ended the previous evening, the kitchen was already dark and Maestro De Lellis, surprised to find the lights turned off when he returned from the *conservatoire*, had looked for us, first in the salon, then in the other rooms, and only finally in the kitchen. We had not heard him, and I was forced to make up some excuse for him – and above all, back home, for Maddalena.

She stopped and looked at me with a solemn expression on her face.

Then she sat on the sofa, spreading her white dress out around her.

"It's frightfully simple: when you were born, your mother fell ill with depression. It happens to most women: nothing new. The hormones at work for nine months have worn themselves out to build life cell by cell, tissue by tissue, and when the work is done they let go. Then it gets better. There usually is a husband who knows what to do at that time, or some grandparents. Your mother had neither. And nor did I – but I did have my music. I always say to Aliberto that he has another mother, as well as me. Anyway,

Erminia could not believe her luck when she was able to regain her place close to your father because your mother was unwell. Your grandparents found your mother's unhappiness too much to bear: they died one after the other – of course they were also quite old. But before dying, they spent days and weeks insulting your father."

"Why?"

"Because your mother had been a happy girl, and now she no longer was."

"What about me?"

"Fear makes people selfish and blind and deaf. No-one could really see you."

"Because I'm ugly."

She made a gesture of annoyance: "You are special, my child. So special that your looks would not have played such a huge part in a different environment. Your father is a doctor. Many things can be done!"

I could not understand, and she saw that.

"I mean little operations, cures to make one better, as everyone does, you know, everyone. And then, enough! We are on earth all of three days, and spend them building hells for each other with all this nonsense about looks and appearances."

She took a deep breath.

"They hid you away. And they hid your mother away too. In a town like ours, these things meant shame and guilt. Things that must be buried away unconfessed. But now, play me some Bach. I need structure."

She stood up and opened the window. The wind wafted in a faraway perfume of incense.

"They are cleaning up at the Basilica of the Virgin, with the doors open," Signora De Lellis says, inhaling deeply again. "It's airless down here."

"What guilt?" I ask.

"They said your mother had discovered a relationship between Erminia and her brother. It was not true, but Erminia did nothing to refute the rumours. She was playing, she liked them to believe it. They said your mother had gone mad because of that, and also that you were Erminia's daughter, and that your mother's pregnancy had been a cover-up. They said she was offered money, that she accepted because of her great poverty, and then lost her mind. It was crazy, of course, completely crazy. I know what people are capable of in this town – oh, I do know! But I had my music. That's why I used to take Aliberto on tour with me. When, as a tiny baby, he could not sleep, I would place him in his basket on the piano lid: after a few bars he was gone. And when I came back, I came with success. Success is a very powerful instant bleach: everything is white and clean again."

"In the diary, my father is 'the liar'," I say as I softly work my way through one of the "English Suites".

"Lies, hypocrisies, evil talk. The Ten Commandments should be rewritten so as to order people ten times over to hold their tongues, rather than worrying so much about sex and private property. Your father had not told your grandparents the truth. There had in fact been some cases, some problems in his family. It's one of the oldest families in town, and they had intermarried for centuries – because of money, of course – and they gave birth to all sorts of creatures, all sorts. Especially half-wits, as they used

156

to be called. Your grandparents would never have allowed him to marry your mother, never. He was scared he would lose her. She was told at the hospital: a secret like a hairball she had to swallow. Offered by Madama Erminia.

"But Aunt Erminia seems to be fond of me."

"Yes, she does. But where is she now? What is she doing for you? You were her audience, the excuse she needed to remain in your house, next to him. Erminia has given her whole self up to her relentless fire. She is not well, Rebecca."

"What about my father?"

"Your father has a good heart, but is like a King Charles spaniel puppy finding himself by mistake in a litter of wolves. He cannot behave as one of his own kind, he cannot follow the ways of the wolves. Inadequate. A victim."

She had spoken with her back to the window, the breeze lifting her fine hair.

I had finished playing a while earlier and was looking at her.

"How do you know all this?" I ask in the end.

"Your mother," she says softly. "Night after night, month after month, year after year."

"But then she wasn't . . ."

"Mad? Oh, yes, she was – in the end she was. Anyone would go mad in her situation, anyone. But in her words it was possible to distinguish truth, to tell it apart from fantasy and from the hypocrisies that surrounded her. It takes patience – and I do have patience. Besides, I am an expert in hypocrisies."

Thirty-five

After my birth, my mother's life had tilted onto a slanted plane. She had not even been able to fight. No-one had taken hold of her hand from above or thrown her a line. Because of selfishness, impossibilities, inadequacy. In her deformed inner world, my father was the liar whose mannered and powerless love only resulted in locking her inside the circle of her own derangement, and he was therefore punished with silence.

Perhaps it had only started as a provocation, a game that had then imprisoned the player without a knight in shining armour to challenge and break the spell. My father had stayed close to her, but the words struggling to find their way into my mother's mind every evening had failed to touch her heart. What use the world of others when our own feelings have forsaken us, and all that is left is the injury of deception suffered? Deception inflicted by one who had declared measureless passion but then had stopped short in the face of our pain, by life that had promised and then recanted, by the God we had implored so much only to find him cloaked in indifference.

My mother had confused sorrow with rancour, and had been unable to see her own weakness mirrored in my father's uncertain and respectful tact.

And he had let it happen.

"The young Signora was like the ducks on Lake Fimon, back when hunting was allowed up there," Maddalena says, still holding

Thirty-seven

"There are no photographs," I say to Maddalena.

I had succeeded in making my explorations last through the whole winter. I had opened each and every drawer and box, moved furniture and rugs, cleaned and tidied the room, adjusted here and there the order in which objects had been arranged.

When I encountered the folder of sketches and notes that my mother had assembled while renewing the palazzo in which I lived, I spent more than a month looking through it. She had made pencil drawings of the front of the house and of all the rooms as they were before the works, and committed her plans for transforming the building to delicate watercolours. She did not have permission to make structural alterations, and so she had worked on the fixtures, furnishings and plants. There were seven watercolours of the main door, showing a sequence of progressive simplifications. In the last one, the door was as I knew it, but on the right, as in every version, there was a stone planter with a pomegranate tree. I had it placed there in the spring. And I asked my father for the wooden globe that she had planned for the salon – like "a little Coronelli", as she had written in her notes. It stood in the corner overlooking the river, framed by the two French windows, the pale marbled walls in the background. And there were watercolours of the smaller and larger balconies, overflowing with lavender and white daisies. She had painted the lavender with tiny silvery brush strokes, and the blue of its flowers shaded into the white of the daisies making a frieze of light that softened the severity of the stone building.

"No," Maddalena says. "No photographs."

"Why not?"

"Some photos are like ladders in a pair of tights: if they're there, you can't look at anything else."

I insist. "Do you know if there are any photographs in the house at all?"

"There are none. Not even of my own: it's in the contract, too."

"What contract?"

"My employment contract: I do not have permission to show any photographs of my family or of any other subject anywhere in the house – that's what it says, in black and white."

"But your photos are . . . a different matter."

"At the interview I had cried all the time. Madama Erminia said I was gushing enough already."

Undaunted, that evening I questioned my father, who explained that Aunt Erminia had preferred things that way: for my mother's sake, as she had said. Better to hide anything that would remind her of what she had been, so as not to make her depression worse. We would show the pictures again when she got better. No, he did not know whether she had kept them or thrown them away. No, he did not know where Aunt Erminia was. He did not think she had stayed in town. She had not been seen at the *conservatoire* in a long time.

I realised then that my house was completely devoid of any memory of the past. There were no pictures or photographs of my mother or my father or my grandparents. Or a lamp that might have belonged to an uncle and then have been carefully restored because it was just perfect for the little table in the hall. Not one rug or a pair of opera glasses, no jewellery passed from mother to daughter all the way down to the house on the river. Among my mother's things I had not found a tiny box hiding in its velvet lining a pair of weightless golden earrings with a finely crafted little crown of blue gems, nor a tiny diamond placed on top of a slender, pointed silver ring. I had looked for that little box. But my mother's jewels had disappeared: hidden, stolen, sold, thrown out of the window and into the river.

That spring the mayor decided to have the murky Retrone drained, because the citizens of Vicenza were complaining of the noxious smells rising from the water. In the mud and silt dredged up by the diggers, the workers found enough refuse to pave the Piazza dei Signori, including a lovely tricycle that turned out to be yellow and green after a good clean. Then came a grandfather clock in walnut wood, still in good condition, and a bag of jewels – not the real thing, albeit very good imitations. The theft – but they were real jewels, the owner had said – had been reported the year before by Mr Longhella, antique dealer in Piazza del Mutilato. There was also a delightful tin caddy decorated with dreamy cupids, perfectly sealed and full of love letters that turned out to have been written by the previous canon of the cathedral to the pretty wife of the current mayor. Having landed the mayor in the pillory and the antique dealer in prison for fraud, the drainage works were promptly declared complete by the town hall, especially as the noxious smells had grown worse and the citizens were making even more noise.

"This town is like its river," Maddalena says as we watch the departing diggers from the balcony of my mother's room. "Better not dig down to the depths."

No coffer of old jewels was ever found.

Thirty-eight

Now I would walk up to the nettle-tree house laden with my discoveries, and Signora De Lellis listened, moving her head backwards and forwards a little or shaking it as if to chase away a bothering thought. Then, in swift episodes, she would regale me with her own memories:

"At night, as she sat on the bench in the street between the two rivers, your mother would speak of this sweet child of hers, named Rebecca. When you were very small, they would sit you on the softest blue cashmere blanket, moving it from room to room to keep an eye on you. They would surround you with toys and teddy bears larger than you were, and you would look around like a fledgling penguin, tiny, your hair like a spiky little crown of black feathers. And she would talk about her own self chained to the rock of her dark sickness, stranded on an island that was near enough for her to see you but too far for her to reach out and touch you, her soul dripped dry by each look that your eyes did not dare give her. She would speak of her own lips, heavy as stone, that could not tell you the story of Prince Charming because she knew that there are no princes and that stories can hurt so much. And your voice was like an unheard song. She could see your uncertain steps, and she really had wanted to stretch her arms out and to support you and stop you from falling. And not only support you, but hold you in her arms and take you upstairs in the evening with laughter and little bouncing steps, and lightly place you on your bed, dizzy with happy flights. But she had not been able to. She had raised her arms, she had stretched them out, oh how she had stretched them! She had thrown herself forward crying out help, help me, my little girl is falling. But the shores of the island on which she was a prisoner had suddenly drawn back, and the water gulf had grown wider and deeper. She had been unable to save you, and everyone around her said she had not wanted to, no-one had seen her raised arms or heard the cry of her will. How could none of them see that water was her enemy?"

Thirty-nine

The end of my last year at secondary school came quickly and found me distracted, unprepared for what would happen next.

I asked my father what could be done about me and he did not understand. About my looks, I explained. A long silence stretched between us. And then he said that yes, he would think about it carefully, something could certainly be done. He did not speak of that again, but the company of that half-promise was enough for me to feel lighter as I climbed the staircase in Contrà Riale, and to sometimes be able to look into my teachers' eyes.

At home I was lovingly tending the lavender and daisies I had planted in large pots and placed on every balcony, just as I had seen in my mother's watercolours. To speed up the final results, I had asked Maddalena to buy large daisies in first bloom, and already the white corollas could be seen, shining luminous against the silvery grey of lavender leaves and the light grey of the stone. Hidden by the parapet as I worked around the plant pots and arranged the daisies so they would spill out over the ledge, I could hear passers-by commenting admiringly on the effect and wondering who might be bringing that old palazzo back to life.

Forty

"I think the most appropriate decision, and surely the best for your child, is to stop exposing her to this environment, in which her behaviour is already – how shall I put it – notorious. Though of course, Doctor, we will do everything we can, you have my word, and after all that is in our own interest too, you understand, absolutely everything, as I say, to stop any news of this matter ever spreading. God forbid that anyone outside might ever know. For everyone's sake, and for the sake of each child, too. First and foremost, I have Mrs Albina's word. She was the one who found your child in a – how shall I put it – a very explicit position. And in a place where she was not supposed to be – but we shall not speak of that, of course. Yes, it was the music room: the place the child might have found – how shall I put it – most congenial? And Mrs Tramarini, she is one of our teachers, she was the one who helped Mrs Albina to – how shall I put it – clean the child up, wash her I mean . . . she has also promised to be very careful with her words. She told me she is one of your patients, and that she has very much respect for you, very much gratitude. As for the other children – leave them to me! I know how to deal with them, how to ensure their silence. They are only a few days away from their final secondary school exams: none will speak now. And none will speak later: they will forget, I know they will. I know them very well. Children forget everything, they have a whole life in front of them! And for them too, it's a question of respect: they know your child is a – how shall I put it – a special case, yes, really a special case. And that is why they have always treated her normally, as confirmed by the fact that I have never received any complaints, either from you, or from the child, of course, and she is here, she can confirm that. The children too understand that it is her – her particular nature that has brought her to behave in that way. But on the other hand you do understand that this is an educational environment. Parents entrust us with their children and we must indeed ensure that they are well respected. That is due to everybody. And for that reason, your child too must tell the truth, of course. That is also a form of respect, as must be very clear. She did entice them. And in fact there has been a certain effrontery in the child's behaviour of late, as you must have noticed? A certain brazen attitude that was – rather extraordinary, in fact. All the children in her class are well-behaved. All from good families: you will certainly know most of them. And there were girls in the room as well. You understand, Doctor, that if there were any truth in what your child is saying, well, she could have cried out: Mrs Albina would have heard her from the bottom of the stairs, just as she saw everyone leaving the music room afterwards: she had been there for ten minutes, she says. From halfway through the break, so as to check that the children would take care on the staircase, you know how they are always running up and down. And of course she would have gone up to the room, as in fact she did afterwards: slowly and heavily, as you understand, poor woman. But the child did not cry out, did not call out. She had enticed the others, out of some . . . some impulse, I mean. You are a doctor, you will understand this kind of thing. And seeing that she had not got what she wanted, she staged a crisis and began to roll on the floor, just as she was, without – without any clothes on, I mean. And that's where Mrs Albina – poor woman – found her. Now for everyone's sake, you will agree, Doctor, the child will not be . . . reported, I mean. I would never want things to go that far. We want to do what's best for her, as well as for the school and for each child, of course. Truth be told, we might have a small problem: as you must surely know, one of the children is the son of the chief of police, and his father might well demand a formal report against your child – you know how it is, he has precise duties, it's the law. But I have spoken to him on the telephone: it was a matter of taking counsel, of doing the right thing, you understand. And he has assured me that the matter will be kept entirely confidential. Out of consideration for your good name, Doctor. The chief tells me that you have delivered all his children: three, I think, plus the one who is studying here at the school. He's from the South, you know – large families. Consideration also for the school's and everyone else's good name. As you can see there is no . . . no intention to prosecute, I mean. We are here to find the best solution for each and for all. Including your child, you understand. And I dare say, I think with good reason, that it would be appropriate if your child did not sit her final exams here. All we need is a medical certificate from you. The law makes provisions for these cases, as you might know. A visiting examining board will come to your house – that's right, they will come straight to you. It's for her, for your girl's sake, first and foremost. As a man speaking to another, I am sure you understand, Doctor."

Forty-one

"But what ac-tual-ly-hap-pen-ed in that room, Rebecca?"

Lucilla has stood up. She is sitting on the little stone balcony outside one of the French windows in the salon, swinging one leg and flicking the ash from her cigarette into the river. The tight skirt hugs her hips and waist, the shirt she is wearing seems to be on the point of bursting at the breast, the only memory left of the abundant shape she had as a child. There is something in her body that speaks to me, but I cannot tell what it is.

She becomes aware of my gaze:

"Since losing weight I've been unable to wear anything properly comfortable. It's like some sort of revenge. What happened, Rebecca?"

I am thinking that she calls me Rebecca, just like Miss Albertina had done, just like Signora De Lellis does.

Forty-two

"What about you?" I say, trying to buy time.

Lucilla crushes her cigarette into the ashtray she has placed on the ledge, then slides down and turns to look at the river, rocking backwards and forwards slightly on her spiky high heels. I recall her as a child, practising in front of the mirror, and think she is much better at keeping her balance now.

"After what happened, we moved to England, and went to live in York. My mother wanted somewhere far away, and thought she would find work as a translator. But she got a job in a cake shop instead, and now she has set up on her own."

"She used to create marvellous cakes," I say to fill the pause. "Angel cake with rose marmalade. Does she still make that?"

"It's her speciality. Her shop is called *Heaven's Drops* – a bit kitsch, but then so is she after all, don't you think? We moved to York after the trial. My mother got away with self-defence. What do you know about me?"

"Nothing," I say. "I've been asking Maddalena for years. But she wouldn't say a word. I don't know anything at all."

"They wouldn't believe me, and so they decided my mother had pushed him into the river in self-defence."

"Did you do it?" I say, and even as I ask I realise that I have always known: she was always the one to solve problems.

"Yes. But the ex-perts testified that I-was-too-small, that I could never have been strong enough to push him off the balcony. They

174

all thought I wanted to protect my mother. I screamed it out with-all-my-strength, that I'd done it myself. My mother in turn was screaming that I was crazy, that I had always made things up. I even grabbed one of the experts by the legs to show him how I did it. They had to give him thirteen stitches – right here, across the back of his head: I'd sent him crashing into the police filing cabinet. But that was no use."

Lucilla turns around and opens her arms, as if to surround the former shape of her body: "They don't know how much strength a fat, desperate child can have."

"Why?" I say.

"Because he-was-aw-ful. Because I'd make the world a better place."

Lucilla pauses and breathes deeply, inhaling the mouldy smell that rises from old river weeds at summer's end.

"He wanted to come back into our lives. He was my father, he said, and that gave him some rights. And also because he'd hit my mother so hard in the belly that she could not get back up from the floor, and I thought she had died. That's why she got away with self-defence."

She looks at me and shakes her blonde hair: she wears it sleek and short these days. I am thinking that it offsets her sharpened features and gives her a refined, aristocratic look.

"Miss Albertina went away too," I say.

"She did. To escape from here. Too much gossip, see? She has always helped us. But she is not very far from us – didn't you know? She is head of a school in this province. She is ex-traor-din-ari-ly good."

"At primary school she saved my life," I say.

"Yes. Mine too. My mother would never had pulled through without her: lawyers, defence, somewhere to stay. She even found her the job in York. I went to college in England."

She pauses again, looks at me with the amused air that she took on when, back in school, she must ab-so-lu-tely tell me about something just when Miss Albertina was in the middle of a lesson.

"I studied singing," she says in the end.

"Singing! Your passion for Schubert's *Lieder*!"

"That's right. Soprano. And I did learn German in the end. After the diploma I worked for a few months with a small baroque music ensemble. A few concerts here and there, then we disbanded: different directions. At the moment I'm unemployed – or 'between jobs', as they say in England."

I look at her and realise what I had sensed in her new look: she had the bearing typical of classical singers, that way of arranging the whole body around the gift of the voice, the shoulders slightly rounded to protect it, the breast generously offered to sustain it.

"I've always been here," I say.

"I know. I know ev-ery-thing about you."

"Did your Aunt Albertina tell you?"

"Yes, she did – and Maestro De Lellis too."

"You know him!"

"Not directly. Aunt Albertina does, though: she got in touch with him after leaving. So she could always have news . . . of you."

"But he's hardly . . ."

"A chatterbox? That's true. But my aunt has a way with people.

And in any case they did . . . well . . . understand each other, if you see what I mean."

"That's where the Maestro went when I was watching over his mother!" I say in amazement, recalling the many days I had spent in the villa over the last few years, being company for Signora De Lellis.

"Yes: he didn't want to upset her, in her condition, he said. But things will be easier now: I know my aunt is applying for a transfer back to the city."

I had kept in touch with Maestro De Lellis. After my final diploma in piano, I would often visit his house to play music with him. Signora De Lellis loved listening to us: she would glide around the room, her eyes half closed, following thoughts that her son believed to be uncertain and vague – but I knew better, and poured all my soul into those afternoons dedicated to her.

With Maddalena, I had helped her through the brief illness that took her from us in the end. And I still walked up to the nettle-tree house to visit and play music, but it had never occurred to me to ask Maestro De Lellis for news of Lucilla, because I was unaware of his relationship with Miss Albertina.

Darkness was falling over the Retrone, and a smoky scent already carrying an intimation of autumn came from the hills and spread densely over the water. In the hillside woods, farm workers were burning dried summer branches.

"Why did you never look for me?" I say, thinking of how the need for Lucilla's presence has cut me like a flesh wound thousands of times in the past years.

"I wasn't ready to come back. Too much sorrow, even for strong Lucilla," she says, smiling as she lights another cigarette. I am thinking that she should not smoke.

"Many singers smoke – and anyway, these are the lightest." She responds to my thoughts, just like she did in the past.

"What about now?"

"A year ago, in London, I thought I recognised your playing: it was the film on the post-war years in Germany – 'Weimar', it was called. One of the main characters was listening to a concert from his favourite pianist, she was playing 'Gaspard de la nuit': it was instant intuition, the way the pianist ended the piece just a fraction too sharply, like you would. But I had never heard you play that piece, and I thought it was just a moment's nostalgia on my part. Then last week I saw the film on Lili Boulanger and immediately realised that only you could play her music that way, those pieces so full of beauty and sorrow – and when you played 'Pour les funérailles d'un soldat' I was ab-so-lu-tely certain: your way of eluding conclusion by sliding away in a rush of notes. And I also saw that the hands were yours. But your name was not in the credits."

"I don't want it there. I have a stage name."

"And so I asked Aunt Albertina, and she asked De Lellis, and then I knew. He had never told us."

"It was a secret. I have my work. It was the last present from the old Signora."

"The old Signora?"

"Signora De Lellis. She really had been very famous, and knew the right people. She said I am not at liberty to keep my . . . talent to myself. So I lend my music to film actresses, when they play the part of pianists."

"Your hands too," Lucilla says.

"My hands too."

"You will have to travel – for the recordings . . ."

"Perhaps. So far only in Italy – but yes, that will come."

"And how do you like it?"

"It's work, but it's lovely. It feels good, and allows for a little dreaming."

"She didn't have Pick's Disease, did she?"

"No, she didn't."

"Aunt Albertina says her son always suspected as much."

Forty-three

"They made me take my clothes off while they stood in a circle around me. I was shaking so much I could hardly move, so it took me much longer than they'd thought. Then I closed my eyes and imagined I was back at your house, listening to 'The Flying Dutchman', you trying at the top of your lungs to sing the German words in the last act, when Erik desperately cries out to his beloved Senta as he is about to lose her: 'Was musst' ich hören! Gott, was musst' ich seh'n! Ist's Täuschung? Wahrheit?' Is it illusion or truth? And Senta throws herself into the sea, singing, vowing faithfulness to the Dutchman doomed to eternal restlessness, 'Preis deinen Engel und sein Gebot! Hier steh' ich, treu dir bis zum Tod' – faithful unto death. In my head, the music was covering the voices all around and I could no longer hear a word they said, until some liquid was splashed in my face, but it got mixed in with the water that swallowed up the loving face of Senta as she sank beneath the waves."

"My God, what was it?"

"Orange juice."

"Orange juice?" Lucilla repeats, and I can sense a smile breaking through her surprise and relief.

"That's right. I had my eyes closed, perhaps they were trying to make me open them, I don't know."

"Orange juice – unbelievable. That's why you were dirty."

"Yes. I must have actually sung out those German words

I hardly knew, and they took fright. And besides, the break was nearly ended by then. So they all ran off, but I didn't realise, and started rolling on the floor. A moment later Albina the beadle came up and found me."

Forty-four

"In short, they thought God-knows-what had happened, and covered everything up," Lucilla says as she lights another cigarette.

"That's right."

"What did your father do?"

"He took me home, and we never spoke of it again. He sent the medical certificate the headmaster wanted, and a few teachers came to our house so I could sit my exam. Maddalena was always with me."

"And then?"

"That summer I went to stay with Signora De Lellis for a few weeks. The Maestro had agreed to hold some summer courses abroad for the first time, precisely because he knew I would keep his mother company. Maddalena came every day to cook and help around the house. And so Signora De Lellis gave up her play-acting with her too, and she spoke and spoke, for days and weeks, and told us everything. Maddalena was crying, I was listening."

"But she never stopped acting the sick mother with her son," Lucilla says pensively.

"No, she didn't."

"Do you know why?"

"Yes, I do: she wanted to protect him, and avoid having to tell him who his father was."

"Do you know?"

"Yes, I do."

"I have learnt to keep secrets by now," Lucilla says, and I recognise her old, familiar curious self.

"It was his grandfather. Signora De Lellis's father. He was drunk and never even realised, and she loved her son too much to tell him. Only a love like that can heal wounds like those."

"Good heavens!"

The expression I had always heard from her mother moves me much more than I would like it to.

"One day my father had a talk with Maddalena, and then went away," I say, resuming my story.

"Yes, my aunt told me. But why?"

"Because he was feeling totally inadequate, as he said to her. He did not know how to protect me, just as he had not known how to protect my mother. Maddalena said that he had kept quiet before the headmaster so as to avoid exposing me to the world, perhaps even to a trial against those kids. He had wanted to spare me further sorrow, as he said."

It was night time by now. The river was silent. The faraway sounds of the *Festa degli Oto* came muffled by the dense mists of autumn.

"Maddalena has stayed with me. My father gave her authority over everything. I know she consulted him now and again, if I got ill or if there were some papers to sign or some expensive decisions to make. I studied at the Istituto Cavanis because it was far from here, travelling back and forth every day. Maddalena drove me until the time when I could go on my own. Then in the afternoons, the *conservatoire* and Signora De Lellis. Until the final diploma in piano."

"What about the town?"

"The town has forgotten everything. The waters have closed over, as Maddalena would say."

"And your father – where is he?"

"I don't know."

"Jesus, you must hate him."

"No: hatred is a feeling I don't know. Hatred is for those who don't understand. I think I can understand him: he's just . . . *sfumato*, as you would say of a musical piece that is too soft and must fade away."

"What do you mean?"

"I am ugly . . ."

"You are ex-traor-din-ari-ly more beautiful these days!" Lucilla interrupts. "Your father did help you in the end, as he had promised."

"Not him. With Maddalena's help, I spoke to some surgeons and redressed some of the simpler things: my right eye, the facial hair. A few things. In any case I am ugly, though I know I could live a different life if I were more of an extrovert, and better able to forget myself and my looks. But I can't do that, and so I live like this, locked up in here until the sun goes down, doing work that allows me to stay hidden. My father is very handsome, but like me he is unable to face the world. He would like to, but just can't, and for that reason I understand him. I am not un-happy, really I am not. I am fine in myself. And I'm not as lonely as an opera singer accustomed to an audience might imagine. I have Maddalena. I have Maestro De Lellis. I have my work contacts. No, this is my life."

Forty-five

"You can stay here if you like," I say to Lucilla. "The house is mine now."

"I have a little girl," she replies.

"A little girl?"

"Yes. Her name is Rebecca."

"Rebecca!"

"She's three years old. I call her Rebby."

"And do you also have . . . a man?"

"No. He lit out the morning after. I was still . . . fat, back then."

"Will she be . . . frightened of me?"

"Don't talk nonsense."

"Are you sure?"

"Pos-itive."

"Then you can both stay here."

I have never used my mother's perfume. I keep the bottles in my room, and little Rebby plays with them, turning them into circles of fairies dancing in rings. A few days ago she broke one. The whole house was flooded with scent.

Author's Acknowledgements

My thanks to the Premio Calvino. Each year, a beautiful world of people who love the written word generously gives of its time in order to read and read, searching for narratives that may be shared with those who move in the world of books.

They have given this novel their recognition.

Rebecca lives in the neighbourhood of Le Barche, at the foot of the hill which is home to the sanctuary of the Virgin of Monte Berico, whose festival the town celebrates each year on the 8th of September. This is the *Festa degli Oto,*[*] which in my mind's eye opens and closes the story.

[*] *Translator's Note:* "oto"= "eight" in the local dialect.

MARIAPIA VELADIANO studied philosophy and theology at university and now works as a teacher. *A Life Apart* was the winner of the Premio Calvino, a prize for unpublished writers. It went on to be shortlisted for the Premio Strega, the most prestigious Italian literary prize.

CRISTINA VITI is a translator and poet whose published work includes translations of Guillaume Apollinaire and Elsa Morante.